BLOOD OF THE BROKEN

ATLANTIS LEGACY BOOK FIVE

LINDSEY SPARKS

RUBUS PRESS

Also By Lindsey Sparks

ECHO WORLD
ECHO TRILOGY
Echo in Time
Resonance
Time Anomaly
Dissonance
Ricochet Through Time

KAT DUBOIS CHRONICLES
Ink Witch
Outcast
Underground
Soul Eater
Judgement
Afterlife

FATELESS TRILOGY
Song of Scarabs and Fallen Stars
Darkness Between the Stars

LEGACIES OF OLYMPUS
ATLANTIS LEGACY
Sacrifice of the Sinners
Legacy of the Lost
Fate of the Fallen
Dreams of the Damned
Song of the Soulless
Blood of the Broken
Rise of the Revenants

ALT WORLD ONLINE
AO: Pride & Prejudice
AO: The Wonderful Wizard of Oz
Vertigo

THE LAST VAMPIRE QUEEN
Heir of Blood and Moonlight
Guardian of Blood and Shadow

THE ENDING WORLD
THE ENDING SERIES
(writing as Lindsey Fairleigh)
The Ending Beginnings: Omnibus Edition
After The Ending
Into The Fire
Out Of The Ashes
Before The Dawn
World Before

THE ENDING LEGACY
World After
The Raven Queen

For more information on Lindsey and her books:
lindseysparks.com

Join Lindsey's mailing list to stay up to date on releases
AND to get access to her FREE starter library:

https://lindseysparks.com/landers/subscriber-library

Playlist

These are the songs that inspired me while while I wrote this book, in no particular order.

You can also listen to the playlist on Spotify:

spoti.fi/3Q8vwda

The War SYML
Don't Know Who I Am Rebecca Roubion
I'm Tired, You're Lonely Liza Anne
Black Sea Natasha Blume
Luci ZAND
World on Fire Klergy
Devil Like Me Akine
Fade to Blue I Of The Storm
Round Here Counting Crows
Sirens Fleurie

Become the Beast Karliene

Ghost Natasha Blume

In Flames Digital Daggers

I Love You, But I Need Another Year Liza Anne

The Deep PHILDEL

The Wolf in Your Darkest Room Matthew Mayfield

Man or Monster Sam Tinnesz, Zayde Wolf

Don't Follow Shelby Merry

Who Are You SVRCINA

Fantasies Llynks

Throne Saint Mesa

Genesis Ruelle

Bedtime Annie Eve

Blue Blood LAUREL

Every Man Is a Warrior Lena Fayre

Warfare Katie Garfield

All the King's Men The Rigs

Weight of Everything ill Factor, Katie Garfield

Game of Survival Ruelle

Take Me to Church MILCK

Subscribe to my newsletter for a detailed list of the songs and the scenes they correlate with from the book:

www.authorlindseysparks.com/join-newsletter

1

As I strode down a corridor in the Med Sector, tension coiled through me, tightening the muscles of my shoulders and neck until my head throbbed. But the physical pain was nothing compared to the ache in my chest. The knot in my gut. The fist lodged in my throat, making each breath a conscious effort.

I rounded a corner, then another, making my way back to the recovery pod where Emi was recuperating from the gut wound she had suffered at the hands of the asshole space pirates. My hands balled into fists as I thought of them. *Despised* them. Every devastating thing that had happened—all the Zari psychics who had died during the attack, all the damage to the *Elysium*, and, of course, Raiden's heroic sacrifice—directly tied back to the pirates. This was their fault. All of it. And there was nothing I could do about this simmering rage because they were already gone.

I forced my fists to unclench and stretched out my fingers. What was done was done. The dead were gone, but there was still hope for Raiden. In a matter of minutes, I would deliver news to Emi that would give her hope of seeing her son again, but it also carried the potential to destroy her completely.

We had found the pirate's shuttle—the ship Raiden had piloted as a decoy to lead the Tsakali scout ship off our trail. Barely an hour ago, the *Elysium's* deep space telemetry system pinged the shuttle's unique signal on Othrys, a once habitable planet orbiting the star Acheron that just so happened to be the Tsakali home planet. Since the shuttle was already logged in our system, it was easier for us to find it, though the signal was extremely spotty.

I wasn't blinded by hope. The location was significant. How—why—of all the places in the universe had Raiden's ship, the decoy that saved the rest of us by drawing the Tsakali off our trail, ended up *there*?

It had been a suicide mission. It *should* have been *my* mission. But Raiden had taken advantage of my weakened state and overpowered me.

My hands balled into tight fists once more, and again, I had to force them to unclench. I shook out my arms and my shoulders. I rolled my neck, attempting to dispel some of the sudden agitation, replacing thoughts of those last devastating moments with Raiden in the transport hanger with everything Hades had told me about Othrys. Dwelling on what had already happened wouldn't help us now, but being prepared couldn't hurt.

As far as we knew, Othrys had been abandoned by the Tsakali millennia ago. It was their home planet, the same world they had abandoned with my people's help tens of thousands of years ago. *Before* the war. Even then, the radiation cocktail emitted by the planet's red star, Acheron, had been making Othrys increasingly uninhabitable for organic life. It had only intensified in the millennia since.

We were already experiencing the power of that radiation, which was causing electromagnetic interference, periodically disrupting the signal from Raiden's ship. Its beacon kept winking in and out on the navigation chart. Of course, that same radiation was what Hades claimed would hide us from detection when we dropped out of FTL in the shadow of Othrys' moon.

I paused outside the door panel leading into Emi's recovery pod and thought through what I was going to tell her. What if we found Raiden's ship but not Raiden? What would be worse—finding a body or finding nothing at all? If we didn't find him on that planet, would the hope that he was still out there become all-consuming?

Already, my internal risk scale was dangerously uneven. Despite Hades' willingness to fly the *Elysium*—the vehicle ferrying the last vestiges of the human and the Olympian races across the universe—into what was most likely a trap of some kind, I knew he didn't think it was the right move. But he was willing to do it. For me.

I pursed my lips and stared at the polished silver surface of the door panel. The knot in my belly tightened, twisting until it was hard to breathe. Was this a mistake? What if going after Raiden led to the destruction of everyone else—all the people stored in the Vault of Souls living out their incorporeal lives in a simulated world? What if I lost Emi because of this mission? Or Fiona or Meg? What if I lost my mom? Or Hades?

I reached out, gripping either side of the doorframe, and closed my eyes. I bowed my head, drawing in shallow, shaky breaths. I could still turn back. I didn't have to tell Emi about the signal. We didn't *have* to follow it to Othrys. It wasn't a *necessary* risk.

When we dropped out of FTL in the Acheron system, we could jump away as soon as the FTL drive recharged. Hades and I knew about the signal, and through our bond, Meg knew, too. Nobody else was aware of where Raiden's ship had landed. Nobody else knew we had found him. Or, at least, that we had found his ship.

I could turn around and head back to the Bridge. I could tell Hades this rescue mission wasn't worth the risk. Raiden gave his life to save us. To give us the chance to reach the safety of Terra. He absolutely *would not approve* of a rescue mission that put everything he sacrificed himself for at risk.

His voice whispered through my mind, a memory of him threatening to tie me to a bed to prevent me from doing something reckless. But those words felt like they were from another lifetime, though they had been spoken barely a month before leaving Earth.

I couldn't make myself turn around. I couldn't abandon him. He hadn't sacrificed his life for the billions of souls on board the *Elysium*; he had done it to save *me*. To prevent *me* from flying that decoy ship away.

Because he loved me.

Anger surged within me, irrational and potent. I was furious with Raiden for putting me in this position. For forcing me to make this impossible choice. The guilt sparked by that anger only enraged me further.

On the off chance that Raiden was still alive out there, I couldn't abandon him.

I inhaled a deep, steadying breath. Another. After the third, I straightened and released the door frame. I pressed the button on the small control pad set into the wall beside the door, and the metal panel slid open.

I froze with one foot in the recovery pod. Emi wasn't in her recliner. A quick scan of the seven other empty recovery chairs spaced out in two neat rows on either side of the room confirmed that Emi wasn't there.

As I moved closer to her abandoned recliner, I noted that Raiden's consciousness orb was gone, but Emi's unused comms patch lay on the tray, still affixed to its backing. Eyes narrowing, I raised my hand to press a fingertip to my own comms patch stuck to the skin behind my ear. I murmured my mom's name to form a private connection with her.

"Mom," I said, my voice low. "Are you awake?" I held my breath, releasing it in a sigh when no response came. She was probably asleep.

I touched my comms patch again, this time forming a link with Hades. "I don't suppose Emi is with you?" I asked him. I had left him on the Bridge only fifteen minutes ago, so I knew he would still be up.

"She's not in her recovery chair?" he asked, responding immediately. His question confirmed he didn't have eyes on her.

"No," I said, scanning the pod again.

"I can trace her comms patch," Hades offered.

"Don't bother," I told him. "She left it here."

"Ah," Hades said. He was quiet for a moment. "What would you like me to do?"

I stared down at the tray table attached to Emi's abandoned chair. Had she taken Raiden's consciousness orb to upload him to the simulation? If we *did* find him alive down on Othrys, we would end up with an awkward duplicate situation. The Olympians had strict rules about uploading, cloning, and regeneration that had been created to prevent that exact thing. No duplicates were allowed within the simulation or to move on to another body.

If we uploaded Raiden's backup, then found him alive on Othrys, the living version would be forever locked out of the simulation. Duplicate consciousnesses threatened the integrity of the entire system, endangering every single person stored within a consciousness orb in the Vault of Souls. Which meant that when Raiden actually died—assuming he still lived—that death would be the end for him.

The prospect disturbed me. But I feared his upload to the simulation for another reason as well.

Again, his voice whispered through my mind. *This is not your fault. It's my choice . . . Promise me you won't blame yourself.* Those had been his last words to me.

The version of him that would be uploaded to the simulation was missing the final hours of his life. I would have to explain to him what happened—why he was being uploaded to the simulation—and I wasn't sure I could recap the events leading to him flying the decoy ship away from the *Elysium* without pointing out all the things I could have done differently to prevent his sacrifice. All the things I *should* have done to stop him from taking my place.

I hated myself for my inability to honor what may have been his dying wish. It was my fault. I *did* blame myself.

I blinked rapidly against the sudden, stinging threat of tears and cleared my throat. "Can you check the Vault of Souls?"

"Of course," Hades said, then fell quiet again.

I stared up at the ceiling, taking slow, controlled breaths to rein in my raging emotions.

"No life signs in or around the Vault of Souls," Hades informed me.

I blew out a breath I hadn't realized I had been holding. I focused on my psychic bond with Meg but knew almost instantly that she hadn't seen Emi recently.

I touched my comms patch again and formed another private connection, this time with Fiona. "Fio? Have you seen Emi recently?"

Seconds stretched out, long enough that I assumed Fiona was asleep as well.

"Aye," Fiona said, finally responding. "I've got her here with me and Stasya in Scout's room. She's assisting the slice and dice on my new toy."

I frowned, wading through Fiona's words and their potential meanings. *Scout's room* was what she and Emi called the lab where we kept the electrified cage housing the creepy, childlike Tsakali scout we had captured on the ice planet. The scout appeared innocent enough now, but I had no doubt that if it got free, it would transform into the vicious creature that had attacked me with razor claws and teeth when we first found it.

"Do you mean the Titan?" I asked, mildly horrified at the thought of the body of the Tsakali psychic who had been working with the pirates being stored in the same lab as the captive scout. The Titan was synthetic, like all Tsakali, so it wouldn't decay, but I couldn't help but sympathize with the scout for having to share a room with one of its "deceased" brethren.

"Obvi."

I frowned to myself. "You're already dissecting her—or, um—it?"

I honestly wasn't sure how the Titans—or any Tsakali—viewed themselves gender-wise. All reference material and recordings I had seen showed Titans with typically feminine curves, but now that I knew their bodies were synthetic, I supposed they could have modeled the

Titans after Olympian psychics—and all Amazon warriors were chromosomally female. Essential characteristics tied to the "y" chromosome intrinsically interfered with psychic abilities.

"Oh yeah," Fiona confirmed. "I couldn't wait to get inside her... give her a little tickle to see what made her tick."

I snorted a laugh, surprising myself, as Fio's inappropriate sense of humor somehow reached through the emotional storm raging within me. I shook my head, snatched Emi's unused comms patch off the tray table, and headed for the open doorway.

"I'm heading to you guys," I told Fiona. "See you soon."

I hurried through the warren of corridors leading from the Med Sector to the Genetec Sector, where the recovery pods and asclypos chambers gave way to an endless string of mostly unused labs, but I couldn't move quickly enough to leave my troubled thoughts behind.

Why was I so torn up about Raiden's likely death? We had an *almost* up-to-death copy of his consciousness. During my lifetimes as Peri, I had lost dear friends many times on missions and had faced no such issues moving on with their regenerated selves. There had never been any sense that the new versions of my friends weren't still *them*. There had never been any sense of loss—merely annoyance at having to wait a couple of decades for their new bodies to grow up and their sense of self to mature into their true selves. This was no different.

Except now, I wasn't just Peri. I had spent two and a half decades as Cora, and new human respect—and fear—for death had been ingrained into my current body's sense of self. Into *my* sense of self. I couldn't shake the feeling that Raiden was likely dead, even though his *self* lived on in a consciousness orb on this ship.

By the time I reached the lab housing the live Tsakali scout—and apparently the now lifeless Titan who had nearly killed me—my jaw ached from gritting my teeth so hard to maintain my stiff upper lip. Unwilling to give myself any more time to waffle emotionally, I punched the button on the control pad beside the door as soon as it was within reach, and the door panel slid open.

Within, Fiona and Stasya stood on one side of the centermost of the three morgue-like lab tables filling the space, Emi on the other, and the Titan's lifeless form stretched out between them. Facing me, Emi held her head cocked to the side, the downturn at the corners of her mouth hinting at disgust as she watched Fiona work. Fiona was literally up to her elbows in the Titan's torso.

In the far corner of the lab, the diminutive scout cowered at the back of its cage. Its eyes were opened wide and unblinking as it, too, watched Fiona dissect the Titan. Was the scout imagining itself laid out on the exam table in the Titan's place? Did it fear such things? Did it *fear*?

The scout's childlike appearance still threw me off. Even though I knew it was likely centuries old, it *looked* like an innocent kid of seven or eight. It was kind of cute. But then I pictured the monster it could transform into, all bulging veins and metal teeth and claws, and goose bumps covered my skin.

I stepped into the room, bracing myself for what I was about to do. As I drew closer and gained a clearer view of the Titan's body—and the crimson staining Fiona's long work gloves—my lips twisted until I was making a full-on ick face. The Titan absolutely did not look like a synthetic being. It appeared to be a woman made of flesh and bone and blood, just like the rest of us.

"I think I've got it . . ." Fiona's features tensed, and she wrenched her arms. Something inside the Titan's body made a crunching sound that reminded me all too well of breaking bone. "There," she said, her expression brightening as the Titan's chest parted down its midsection. She straightened, pulling her arms free with a sickening, squelching sound. "That should do it."

Emi glanced at me, offering me a halfhearted smile. I spotted Raiden's consciousness orb tucked into the nest of Emi's sweater on the next lab table over, where Fiona had set up her hybrid workstation out of human and Olympian tech. Emi returned her focus to Fiona and the dissection.

Fiona, still oblivious to my arrival, wedged her fingers into the narrow opening in the Titan's chest cavity. With a grunt, she pushed the two sides apart, affording us all a better view of the Titan's insides.

"Stasya?" Fiona said as she shuffled a few inches to the left, making room for Stasya to take over holding open the Titan's broken ribcage.

I suppressed a gag. Poor Stasya.

"See this here?" Fiona said, pointing to something around where I would have expected an organic creature's heart to be. "This is the CPU, but this band wrapped around it is what I was talking about on that scan. It reminds me of a superconductor." She angled her head, her loose topknot of neon orange hair flopping to one side. "Or what I would imagine a superconductor would look like if it were grown rather than made," Fiona clarified. "Not that I have any idea of how such a thing would be possible."

"Huh," Emi said, a crease forming between her brows. She gripped her own elbow with one hand and tapped her lips with the index finger of the other. She glanced at the scout huddling in the back of its cage. "Nothing like that showed up on any of the scans we did of that one."

"Right?" Fiona pointed to Emi with one bloodied finger. "I can't help but wonder if this part is unique to the Titans. Like, maybe this is the source of their gifts, like a psychic fuel cell."

Emi's faint frown deepened, and she shook her head thoughtfully. "I suppose, though I don't know how we would test the theory." She looked past Fiona, her focus locking onto me. "Maybe you or Stasya could channel psychic energy into it and see if whatever this is can hold the energy?"

Fiona spun around to face me, flinging gobs of blood in my direction. I instinctively held up a hand and turned my face away. "Gross, Fio."

Fiona glanced down at her gory gloves, then flashed me a sheepish smile. "Sorry, Cora. But what the shite?" she snapped, all hints of contrition vanishing. "How long have you been standing there?" She waved the question away before I could answer. "Never mind. Will you do it?" She glanced back at the half-dissected Titan. "Will you channel into it?"

"If you think it's safe," I said, shrugging. "Yeah, sure." I looked past Fiona to Emi. "But I need to talk to you first, Em." I nodded toward the doorway, figuring she would prefer some privacy for what I was about to tell her.

I had gone back and forth over whether we should tell her the true purpose of the mission to Othrys, not wanting to give her false hope. But Raiden was her son, and if I was going to ask her to delay uploading his consciousness to the simulation, I needed to be honest with her about the reason.

My heart beat faster as Emi followed me back to the doorway and out into the corridor. I turned to her, and whatever she saw on my face caused her to hug her middle.

I forced myself to speak before I could wuss out. "We found Raiden's ship."

Emi gasped and brought a hand up to her mouth, her eyes going glassy.

I licked my lips. "We're on our way there now," I told her. "Hades says we should reach the planet where the ship's signal is originating soon, but—" I winced, bracing myself against the hope welling in Emi's eyes along with all those tears. "There's no guarantee we'll find him there." I forced myself not to retreat from Emi's gutting stare. "Or that he'll be alive if we *do* find him."

Emi closed her eyelids, and tears cascaded down her cheeks. Her shoulders jerked with silent sobs, but I waited for her to regain her composure. If I reached out to her, if I comforted her in any way, we would both lose it completely. We didn't have time for emotional breakdowns right now, not with the impending rescue mission on the horizon.

Finally, Emi inhaled, deep and tremulous, then opened her red-rimmed eyes. "I understand."

2

S ITTING TAILOR-STYLE ON THE metal grating of the observation deck on the top floor of the *Elysium*, I stared out at the stars through the reinforced glass curving along the wall and ceiling. Since the ship currently moved faster than the light given off by all those distant celestial bodies, the stars formed glowing lines streaking through space like multicolored laser beams. I rested my hands on my knees and arched my back, stretching my neck first one way, then the other, earning a satisfying *crack-crack-crack* and a tingling rush of endorphins.

I should have been in my private quarters, catching whatever scraps of sleep I could manage. I needed to be clearheaded and ready to handle whatever awaited us on Othrys.

But every time I even closed my eyes for longer than a blink, I saw Raiden's face peering out at me through the porthole in the hull of the pirate shuttle. I saw his hand pressed against the glass, mine against his, and renewed grief crushed my heart. The one time I did actually drift off, the gut-wrenching goodbye had played out in all its horrifying glory. I had gasped awake, heart hammering and cheeks wet with tears.

That was when I gave up on sleep and fled from my quarters, heading up to the observation deck in the hope that the stars might bring me comfort. I needed this reminder that I was small, that the universe was infinite.

I inhaled deeply, filling my lungs to the brim, then closed my eyes. I pictured darkness. A spark appeared in that black void. I imagined it growing to a flickering flame, beating back my inner demons with its light.

A silhouette appeared at the edges of the darkness. Tall and broad. Familiar.

My heart beat faster, and my chest tightened, my rib cage seeming to constrict around my lungs until my breaths quickened.

The figure stepped forward, and Raiden's face came into view, flickering in the dim light from my flame. He raised his hand like he was pressing it against an invisible barrier. A porthole. His face slowly morphed into another, elongating and sharpening. His hair lengthened and lost its color until it was shoulder length and silver-blond. He transformed.

Raiden no longer stood in my mind's eye. Now, I saw Hades, his stare somber as he mouthed a final goodbye.

I gasped, clutching my chest with one hand, and snapped my eyelids open. Panic cocooned me, its embrace unrelenting. My upper body caved in on itself as I fought for air. My shoulders slumped, and I curled my legs up and hugged my knees.

I dragged my stare up from the metal grating on the floor and focused on the streaming stars, needing this proof that I was here, on the observation deck, not down in the transportation hangar, watching Raiden *or* Hades leave me. The streaming stars provided a visual reminder that

I was on my way to Raiden right now. And Hades was on the Bridge. I was doing everything I could to keep them both safe.

But are you?

The question whispered through my mind, toxic and insidious.

Are you really?

"Stop it!" I hissed through gritted teeth, smacking the side of my head with my open hand. "Just stop it!"

With a low growl, I unwrapped my arms from around my knees and straightened my legs, extending them out in front of me. My hands trembled, my muscles thrumming with unspent adrenaline. I uncurled my body, stretching out on the floor to give my lungs the maximum space to expand.

Panic attacks were nothing new to me. They had been almost a daily occurrence for the past two decades. As I stared out at the streaming stars, the tremors racking my body gradually lessened, giving way to the faint vibration of the ship, and the panic lost its chokehold over me.

My mind wandered in a less disturbing direction. I took note of the sense of wonder sprouting in my chest and of the dichotomy of my own feelings about journeying across the universe. How strange to feel as though hurtling through space at faster-than-light speeds was both novel and mundane. The part of me that had once solely been Cora was amazed, but the part of me that had spent lifetimes as Peri was utterly unfazed. I was no longer two people stuffed into one body, but times like these made me think my two selves hadn't fully integrated into a single identity, either. My sense of self wasn't exactly divided, but it wasn't completely unified.

Like so many things in my life right now, it was *complicated*.

At the sound of a throat clearing behind me, I craned my neck to peer toward the back of the observation deck. Strands of my loose hair snagged on the metal grating, making me wince.

My mom approached, a slight, forced smile curving her lips. The tension in her jaw and around her eyes made me think she was aware of where we were headed.

"I hear we have a new mission," she said as she drew closer, confirming my suspicion. Had Hades told her? Or had Emi? Or perhaps, by now, it was common knowledge.

"Yeah," I whispered, the single word drawn out and utterly devoid of confidence. I crossed one ankle over the other and raised my head off the floor, folding my arms beneath it to use as a pillow.

When my mom reached me, she lowered herself to the floor and bent her legs, drawing them up to rest her forearms on her raised knees. She gazed out at the silvery veil of starlight, her presence a comfort, even in the silence. We sat there for minutes, quietly observing the universe together.

"How are you doing, sweetheart?" my mom finally asked.

My whole body tensed.

"This is an incredibly difficult situation for everyone, but for you . . ." She sighed. "I can only imagine what you're feeling right now."

"I'm fine," I croaked. I cleared my throat and repeated the statement. "I'm fine."

She turned her face toward me, resting her chin on her shoulder.

I glanced at my mom but had to look away under the weight of her measuring stare.

"Have you gotten any sleep since, well . . ." She exhaled a breathy, humorless laugh. "Have you gotten any sleep?"

I blew out a breath and shook my head. "Every time I close my eyes, I see him. I see his face through the glass. I see his lips moving as he tells me—" I choked on the words as anger surged up from the darkest depths of my heart. He had left me behind. He had *left* me.

I squeezed my eyelids shut, but there he was in my mind's eye, mouthing those words.

Promise me you won't blame yourself.

I did, and I didn't. I blamed myself for not making him see I was a worthy partner. A strong ally. I blamed myself for not earning his trust and respect as a warrior. But I blamed him for not believing in me, for not taking me with him to back him up.

I love you. That was the last thing he had said to me before flying the decoy away, effectively sacrificing himself to save everything I loved. Everything but himself. For all I knew, he was dead. Thoughts that we wouldn't find him—or his body—were ever-present in my mind. He might have been captured. Tortured. Killed.

And I was *mad at him*? I had never felt like such a steaming pile of shit before in all my lives.

"Ugh," I growled, opening my eyes again.

I raised my head, pushed off the metal floor with my elbows, then sat up all the way, once again hugging my folded legs to my chest. Turning my face toward my mom, I rested my cheek against one knee. My eyes stung with the threat of tears. If I continued down this mental path, they would flow freely. I knew that, and I didn't want to cry anymore, but I couldn't stop myself from voicing my nagging fears.

"What if he's not there?" I said, my voice weak. "What if I have to spend the rest of forever wondering?" I swallowed roughly, choking on the dread. "Wondering how he died?" My voice wavered, and I drew in a shuddering breath. "In some ways, I'm hoping he's dead because the alternative—that they're holding him captive and *doing things* to him—is so much worse." I stifled a sob and buried my face in the crook of my arm.

"Oh, sweetheart." My mom rested a hand on my shoulder, her touch gentle and reassuring.

"I mean, who does that?" I asked, raising my head to look at her. "Who *hopes* someone they love is dead?"

Sympathy contorted my mom's features. "Oh, Cora," she said, sliding her hand along the back of my neck and curling her arm around my shoulders. She pulled me against her, wrapping her other arm around me and tucking my head under her chin.

I collapsed against her, clutching the front of her sweater as the sorrow, rage, and sheer wretchedness of my existence exploded out of me in a bout of guttural, full-body sobs.

My mom's arms tightened around me. "It's okay, sweetheart," she murmured. "It's all right. I'm here for you. I will always be here for you. Whenever your burdens are too heavy, I will help you carry them," she promised. "Always, my sweet Cora-Borealis."

I laugh-sobbed at the sound of the old nickname.

My mom smoothed down my hair and rocked me gently. "And I will help however I can when we get to Othrys—and after—but please don't get yourself worked up before we know what we're dealing with." Her voice was soft, steady, soothing. "We might very well find Raiden with the ship. And if we don't, Hades tells me most ships record what happens on board, like an alien version of a black box. If Raiden isn't there, hopefully the recording will give us some further insight."

Her logic and reassurance battled against my raging emotions, gradually wrestling them into submission. My sobs lessened as she spoke, and I relaxed my death grip on the front of her sweater.

"But," she added. "If we get to Othrys and find his ship and still don't know what happened to him . . ." She paused like she was considering her words carefully. "If you want to take the *Argo* and follow his trail to find out what happened to him, I will go with you," she vowed. "I'm with you until the end."

Her words echoed in my mind. This mission could very well lead to that exact end.

I squeezed my eyelids shut as tight as I could, welcoming the mental image of Raiden because it was better than picturing my mom suffering a similar fate. Better than considering the danger in which following Raiden's trail even this far was placing her—and everyone else on board the *Elysium*. Better than facing the terrifying truth.

That this might only be the first loss of many.

And in all my lifetimes, death had never felt so permanent.

3

H ADES' GAZE LINGERED ON my face as I ascended the stairs to join him atop the captain's platform on the Bridge. His attention was no real surprise. My face still felt puffy from the cryfest with my mom, and my heart was heavy with the weight of all we were risking by venturing to Othrys. All *I* was risking, because going after Raiden's ship had been *my* call.

The lid cracked open on the lockbox shoved into the darkest corner of my heart, threatening to release those volatile emotions. I had only just managed to stash them away. I wrapped a chain forged from my will around the box. I *would not* break down again. I had neither the time nor energy to waste on such weakness.

I wondered what Hades thought of my tears. Did he believe they had been shed for Raiden alone? Did he have any idea that many sprang from the idea of losing him, as well? My index finger itched to touch the stone glowing a subtle amber in the regulator hanging from the chain around my neck and to unleash my psychic abilities so I could find out.

I clenched my hands into fists and offered Hades a tight smile. "How close are we?"

"Minutes from landing the jump," he said, returning his attention to the oversized holoscreen hovering in front of him.

I climbed the final step and crossed the narrow platform to perch on the wide armrest of his chair. I scanned the windows open on the holoscreen, taking note of their contents. The background displayed a navigation chart, the solid white beacon marking the *Elysium* shifting ever closer to the large, red dot marking Acheron's location on the chart.

On the left side of the screen, a long, narrow window displayed a list, and beneath it, another smaller window displayed a dozen multicolored bars, some half-full, some almost entirely empty. On the right side of the holoscreen, another window displayed an ever-changing line chart with red, orange, yellow, and magenta lines shifting with jagged peaks and deep valleys. A small window had been tucked into the upper right-hand corner, displaying a countdown timer. Just under two minutes until we dropped out of FTL.

"You're sure nobody will be able to detect us?" I asked, glancing at Hades out of the corner of my eye. If his answer was anything other than a definitive *no*, I was calling the mission off.

"I am sure." Hades raised one hand, indicating the fluctuating line chart with a flick of his long fingers. "No tech could differentiate the burst of chaos energy given off by our arrival from that mess of radiation," he explained. "The electromagnetic interference caused by the output of radiation from Acheron will conceal our presence. With our shields and the rebounding radiation, we will be undetectable. I am not uncertain about this."

I studied his face through narrowed lids but found no hints of deception. I turned my attention back to the holoscreen. He wasn't uncertain *about this*. Was he less sure about other aspects of the mission?

A thought struck, and I frowned. "If the radiation will conceal us, couldn't it be concealing other ships that are already there?" I looked at Hades, studying his angular profile. "Like the Tsakali?"

Hades settled back in his seat and leaned his elbow on the opposite armrest from where I was sitting, angling his face toward me. "There is always that risk, but even if other ships are already there, they will not detect our arrival or our lingering presence." His features tensed as he searched my gaze. "Are you having second thoughts about the mission?"

I was. And third and fourth and fifth thoughts. This was not a good idea. Raiden wouldn't have approved. I could picture his scowl so clearly. See the disapproval in his stare. He would cross his arms over his chest and threaten to tie me up until I came around to his way of thinking.

Before I could confess my doubts to Hades, an alarm blared through the ship-wide speaker system. We were about to drop out of FTL. We had arrived.

I reached out, bracing myself on the railing that curved around the captain's platform. Hades lowered his hand to grip the end of the armrest on the other side of his chair. The ship shuddered.

In a blur, the navigation chart reoriented itself to display Acheron's planetary system. The viewscreen spanning the entire front wall of the Bridge flickered, the curtain of streaming starlight vanishing, and then the screen filled with a red inferno. Acheron. My eyes widened as I stared at the viewscreen, at the red behemoth blazing in all its dying glory. I couldn't help but feel like we were flying straight into hell. Or possibly just my own personal hell.

"We can leave," Hades said softly.

I looked at him, stunned speechless by his offer. The mask he had worn for lifetimes was that of the reserved, calculating prince of Olympus, but I knew better. It had taken literal lifetimes for him to let his mask slip, but once he did, once I glimpsed his true nature—generous, compassionate, and perceptive—I had loved him. I *did* love him. But I was putting him at risk, all to take a moonshot at rescuing another man *who I also loved*.

"We can wait for the FTL drive to recharge and jump away," Hades added. "It's not too late."

I swallowed around the lump in my throat. Or maybe that was my heart.

A window popped up in the center of the navigation chart. The red, flashing border around the window drew our attention back to the holoscreen.

Hades leaned forward and reached for the holoscreen, dismissing the warning with a swipe of his hand. I glanced at him in time to see his frown before he blanked his expression.

My eyes narrowed. "What was that about?"

Hades stared ahead, back straight and shoulders stiff, and I could practically see the thoughts racing through his mind as he worked through his response. *Here* was the calculating aspect of his nature in action.

Dread twisted in my gut. What was he hiding?

"Hades," I said, my voice low and threaded with warning.

Hades inhaled deeply, then let out a long sigh, his posture slumping. He raised his hands, smoothing back the silver-blond strands that had slipped free from the band binding his hair at the base of his skull. "We're running low on several essential element cartridges."

My eyebrows rose. Had he been hiding this from me on purpose? Anger sparked to life within me, reigniting the volatility in my veins.

Hades pointed to the two windows on the left side of the holoscreen, one with the list and the other containing a series of multihued bars. "If we hadn't stopped here, we would have needed to find another resource-rich planet soon," he explained. "It just so happens that Othrys is an ideal location to search—formerly inhabited by an advanced civilization, abandoned in a hurry. We'll likely find everything we need there."

I pressed my lips together as I stared at his profile while he pointedly avoided looking at me. "Why didn't you say anything?" I asked, unclenching my jaw to speak.

Finally, Hades focused on me, his ice-blue eyes imploring me to understand. I didn't need access to my gifts to sense how conflicted he was feeling about this. "I didn't want this situation to influence your decision to pursue the rescue mission."

My brow furrowed, and I opened my mouth to argue.

Hades held up a hand, holding off what was sure to be a biting retort. "It wouldn't have mattered in the grand scheme of things," he said. "If you chose to pursue Raiden, then we could search Othrys. If you chose to move on, then we could find another planet to search." His expression softened. "We still can."

My chin trembled as my emotions rattled the lockbox in my heart. I wanted to rage at Hades. Why did he have to be so damn understanding? Why couldn't he be petty or snide or domineering? Why wouldn't he fight me? Try to influence me? Persuade me? Control me?

Because you're his partner, whispered my inner voice of reason. *His equal. Because he respects you.*

I squeezed my eyelids shut. "I don't know what to do," I admitted, my voice barely above a whisper.

"We're already here," Hades said calmly, like his steadfast composure might help regulate my own unstable emotions. "We might as well search Othrys for what we need. It's as good a place as any."

My chin trembled, and I nodded, unable to open my eyes. Unable to speak.

"And while you're down there," Hades added, "you can find the ship."

Again, I shifted my chin down and then raised it back up.

"I've already drawn up a list of all the depleted element cartridges," Hades said, all business now. "I included diagrams and chemical signatures, so your team can use their holobands to discern the correct element cartridges."

I cleared my throat and opened my eyes, focusing on the holoscreen. "That'll be helpful," I said, the words coming out stronger than I felt.

I looked at Hades, placing one trembling hand on his shoulder. "Thank you," I said, hoping he could see that I wasn't just thanking him for his careful preparation for the resupply mission. I was thanking him for the shift of our focus from my reckless rescue mission to one genuinely benefiting the whole ship. And beyond that, I was thanking him for his ability to read me, to instinctively know what I needed.

Hades covered my hand with his. Our stares locked, and my breath hitched. I didn't deserve the way he gazed at me. Eyes stinging, I averted my stare to the wall of fire visible beyond the holoscreen.

A sliver of darkness appeared at the very edge of the viewscreen. As that sliver grew and we moved past Acheron, some of the tension inside me eased. Stars winked into existence, brightening as the hellish glow from the red giant diminished. And then we were past it.

A brighter spot coalesced among the stars, glowing a haunting reddish-orange, slowly growing larger. A planet. Othrys.

My hand still rested on Hades' shoulder, and his still covered mine. I closed my eyes, setting a string of tears free. I was *so sick* of crying, but I couldn't seem to stop.

Hades' fingers curled around my hand, a silent promise of support. An unspoken vote of confidence—in me.

I hastily wiped away the tears, then sniffled, cleared my throat, and lifted my eyelids. Othrys had tripled in size on the viewscreen. I took a deep breath and looked at Hades once more.

He squeezed my hand, the tightening of the skin around his eyes barely perceptible. "We'll enter orbit soon," he said, relaxing his grip. "I'll send drones down to the surface as soon as we arrive."

"Good." I pulled my hand from his shoulder, flexing and clenching my fingers. The sense of his touch lingered, like it had been seared into my skin. "I'll get my team prepped and loaded onto the *Argo*," I said, standing.

I reached the top of the stairs leading down from the platform in two steps, then stopped, turning partway to face Hades. "Thank you," I said again, my voice raspy with emotion.

Hades bowed his head.

I turned away and started down the stairs, walking away from Hades. And toward whatever awaited me on Othrys.

4

S ELENE WAITED FOR ME by the *Argo* in the transport hangar with Caly and five more Zari psychics, including the three who had joined us on the mission to search the debris field surrounding the planet Nykta—Melyse, Kyra, and Helyna. I had yet to work closely with the other two, Zephyra and Lyssa, but both had come highly recommended by Caly, so I felt confident in their abilities.

I focused on the seven women waiting for me, blocking out the invasive memories threatening to break the surface of my conscious mind. The last time I was in the transport hangar, I had watched Raiden fly away. I refused to relive those horrifying moments when there was a chance I could see him again.

Selene and the others wore hoplon suits and sported orichalcum-laced hoods poached from some of the dead pirates. In addition to the dorus sheathed on their backs, each woman had a weapon belt loaded with a pair of laser pistols tucked into the holsters on either side of her hips.

Through the bond we shared, I sensed Meg within the *Argo*, running through the preflight maintenance routine and performing an in-depth systems check to make sure everything was in order for the impending trip to Othrys. The mechanic bots had already repaired what the pirates had damaged when disabling all our ships, but it was standard operating procedure to double-check their work.

Caly caught my eye, raising her chin in greeting. She was in a much better place now that her mom, Ilyana, had been uploaded to the simulation. She had really stepped up, settling into a leadership role among the Zari psychics—the *new* Amazons—despite her youth. Ilyana must have been so proud of her daughter.

I offered Caly a closed-mouth smile and a slight bow of my head as I neared, then turned my attention to Selene. She stood with her arms crossed over her chest, a small drawstring bag gripped in one fist.

My old friend and the only other original Amazon warrior on board the ship nodded to me in greeting. "Now that Cora's here, I have something for each of you," she said, scanning the faces of the five women gathered around her. "Meg," she called toward the *Argo*. "Come join us for a minute."

Caly and Melyse shifted away from one another, making room for me. "Thanks," I murmured.

The clang of boots on a metal floor preceded Meg as she hurried toward the aft of the *Argo* to join us. She trotted down the lowered rear ramp, flashing me a quick smile as Melyse and Kyra shifted apart to make room for her in our huddle.

Selene uncrossed her arms and opened the drawstring bag. She reached inside, pulling out what appeared to be a large, gold locket. It was perfectly round, flat-ish, and nearly filled her palm. All that was missing was a chain.

Selene wedged the tip of her thumbnail into the edge of the object, then flicked her thumb, and it popped open. "This," Selene said, holding the gold locket-like thing out on her raised palm, "is a regulator case."

My brows bunched as I studied the golden object. "What's it for?"

Selene looked at me, her eyes widening in surprise. A moment later, she let out a breathy laugh and shook her head. "I forget that you never had to face the Titans." She tilted her head to the side. "Excluding the recent excitement."

I suppressed a laugh. Only Selene would describe space pirates invading our ship and nearly destroying us all as something so bland as *recent excitement.*

Selene returned her attention to the golden regulator case resting on her palm. "The stones in our regulators are basically extremely diluted chaos fragments," she explained. "They're too weak for any kind of tech or radar to pick up, but a psychic—a *Titan*—can sense one."

"And *this* will prevent any Titans who might be down on Othrys from sensing our regulator stones?" I asked, glancing from Selene to the open case on her palm, then back up at her.

"Exactly." Selene demonstrated fitting her own regulator into one half of the clamshell, then snapped the case shut around it. "Orichalcum-laced gold—just like our hoods—blocks any and all psychic energy." She opened the drawstring bag as wide as it would go and held it out into the center of our huddle with both hands. "Grab one and put it on. This was the Tsakali's home world. There's no way to predict what we might find down there."

I hesitated before fitting the case around my regulator. In this incarnation, I had struggled nearly my whole life with controlling my gift, so much so that for two decades, I had believed it to be a disease. Something that was *wrong* with me. I feared that *not* being in touch with my regulator would revert me to my previous state and render me incapable of controlling my psychic abilities.

This mission was already dangerous enough for all involved. If I was cut off from my regulator and lost control of my gifts, I would be a hazard not only to myself but to everyone on the team. If that were the case, I would need to back out of the mission. A slight tremor racked my hands as I considered leaving these eight women to risk their lives down on Othrys *without me*. My chest tightened, and my breaths grew shallower.

"Won't this also cut me off from my regulator?" I glanced at Selene, who watched me curiously, and my cheeks heated when I realized what I had said. "Cut *us* off, I mean."

Sympathy and understanding softened Selene's stare, and her lips curved into a gentle smile. "That won't be an issue," she said, reaching out to grip my shoulder. "The alloy contains enough orichalcum to conduct psychic energy via touch. So long as the case is in contact with our skin, we will each still be connected to our regulators."

I nodded and stared down at the regulator case in my trembling hand. I slid my thumbnail into the clasp edge, but my hands were shaking too badly to open the case.

Selene stepped in front of me, blocking the others' view of my silent breakdown. She opened the golden clamshell easily, fitted it around my regulator, then snapped the case shut and tucked the now larger pendant into the collar of my hoplon suit.

"We'll find him," she said, withdrawing her hands. "And if he's not there. If there's nothing to find, we will honor his sacrifice by finding the resources we need to refill the element cartridges and completing the mission he gave his life to protect."

She had misread the reason for my wavering resolve, but I nodded anyway. Doubt was toxic. Uncertainty was the last thing this team of Amazons needed when heading into what promised to be a dangerous situation.

I drew in a shuddering breath, reinforcing my conviction to follow through on the mission. This wasn't just about Raiden anymore. This was about supplying the ship with the resources it needed to carry us the rest of the way to Terra.

I ignored the voice reminding me that Raiden wouldn't be okay with this mission. He would want us to move on, to find another planet to search for the resources we needed to refill the element cartridges. Even in his absence, he could make me second guess myself.

After another, steadier breath, I nodded again. We were doing this.

I scanned the women who had fallen back to wait by the *Argo*, watching Selene and me without making it obvious. Their expressions were curious but not wary. They were committed to the mission.

When I had first gathered Selene and all the new Amazons in the training room to propose the recovery mission and ask for volunteers, I had expected opposition. What I hadn't expected was for every single one of them to step forward. To *feel* their support. To have gone from the near-complete isolation of my life on Orcas Island to this sense of community. This sisterhood.

It was overwhelming. And terrifying.

I suddenly had so much more to lose.

"Are you ready?" Selene asked, her voice pitched low, for my ears alone.

I nodded a third time, not yet trusting my voice to be steady.

Selene offered me an encouraging smile, then turned her attention to the gathered team. "All right," she said, clapping her hands together.

"Hoods up and deactivate your regulators. It is highly unlikely that Raiden's ship ending up on the Tsakali home planet is a coincidence. Assume this is a trap. Assume there will be an ambush. Assume the surface is crawling with Titans." She paused, letting her warnings sink in.

I gulped, balling my hands into fists. This was a terrible idea.

"We need to be ready for anything," Selene said, "But psychic powers are only to be used as a last resort. Do not remove your hoods. Period. A Titan will sense your mind the instant it is unshielded, and if she can get close enough to you, she will attempt to forge a connection and drain your psychic energy."

The Amazons' expressions hardened, their spines straightening as they prepared for battle.

"If you perish today," Selene continued, "your backup will be transferred from storage to a consciousness orb, and you will be uploaded to the simulation." Again, she paused, surveying the team. "What awaits us after death?"

"The next life," I murmured automatically, the Amazon mantra ingrained into me from countless repetitions over my many lifetimes.

Selene raised her voice and repeated her question. "What awaits us after death?"

"The next life," the gathered psychics answered.

"What awaits us after death?" Selene practically shouted.

"The next life!" came our booming response.

Selene's lips curved into a wicked smile, most certainly fueled by an adrenaline rush as she prepared to launch the mission. "All right, Amazons," she said. "Let's head out." She marched forward, leading the way up the ramp and onto the *Argo*.

I hung back, bringing up the rear as the team followed her onto the ship. Meg, Caly, and the others settled into their seats along the side of the ship's cabin, preparing for launch by deactivating their regulators and pulling their hoods up over their heads. Selene waited at the top of the ramp by the control pad. She punched a button as soon as I stepped onto the ship, and hydraulics whirred as the ramp raised behind me.

I made my way to the cockpit area at the front of the ship, settling into the rightmost seat. The flight controls were currently aligned with the other seat, which I left for Selene. She currently had the steadier hand and was the far more experienced pilot.

I tugged my regulator free from my hoplon suit, opened the case, and swiped my fingertip around the amber stone to deactivate it. The stone blazed electric blue, and I closed my eyes, focusing on my newly awakened senses. I could only feel two other presences on board the *Argo*—Selene approaching behind me and Meg, who was a constant fixture in my mind, regardless of whether my psychic senses were active or muted. So far as I could tell, nobody else was on the ship with us. I frowned and peeked around my seatback to glance at the women strapped into their seats, impressed by the effectiveness of the pilfered orichalcum-laced hoods.

Meg's gaze caught mine, and concern flooded into me through our bond.

I clamped down on the tether connecting us as tightly as I could. "I'll be fine," I mouthed in silent reassurance.

She pressed her lips together, forming a thin, flat line. She remained unconvinced.

I flashed her a quick smile, then faced forward once more.

Selene settled into the waiting pilot's seat on my left, strapping herself in before deactivating her regulator and securing her hood. She inhaled deeply, then released an audible sigh. Her giddiness was palpable. "I love this part," she murmured. "The anticipation. The unknown." She glanced at me sidelong, her lips curved into a secretive smile. "It's the sweetest rush."

"You're insane," I told her flatly.

She grinned. "Maybe. But at least I'm not boring."

I laughed under my breath and shook my head, then raised a hand to my comms patch to form a private link with Hades. "Hades, we're ready to go," I said. "Are we cleared to launch?"

Hades didn't respond right away. I locked stares with Selene, unease unsettling my stomach. The last time Hades had gone silent over the comms system, he had been knocked out and the Bridge had been taken over by hostiles.

"Hades?" I repeated and held my breath.

"Yes, I'm here," he finally responded.

I relaxed, releasing my breath. "Is there a problem?"

"I'm not sure," he said. "I'm picking up on some strange energy readings from the surface of Othrys."

I chewed on the inside of my cheek, not liking the sound of that one bit.

Selene raised her eyebrows, in the dark on my private conversation with Hades.

I shrugged one shoulder and shifted my stare forward to the viewscreen displaying our clear shot through the transport hangar to the sealed inner airlock door.

"I'm really not sure what I'm looking at," Hades told me.

"Could it just be excess energy from Acheron rebounding off the surface of the planet?"

"Most likely," Hades said, drawing out the two words. "But it's causing a significantly larger amount of electromagnetic interference than I had anticipated," he added. "I've lost contact with the drones."

I narrowed my eyes, reading between his words. "You think we'll be out of reach when we're down there."

"I do," he confirmed.

I felt inappropriately relieved. It was bad news when viewed from any angle save for one: this likely explained why we had lost the signal from Raiden's ship.

I glanced at Selene. "Assume we'll be cut off from the *Elysium* once we're down there," I told her.

"Oh?" Selene said, her eyebrows hiking halfway up her forehead. "Shit."

I inhaled deeply through my nose and turned in my seat as much as I could without unfastening the restraints. "Hades just informed me that we likely won't be able to communicate with the *Elysium* during the mission," I told the psychics, looking at each woman in turn. "I won't hold it against you if you want to back out now."

Meg made a fist and pressed it against her chest, directly over her heart. Through our dampened bond, I could read the meaning of the gesture. She was with me until the end, no matter what.

One by one, starting with Caly, the other six Amazons pressed their fists to their chests.

My own heart seemed to swell until I was practically choking on it. I closed my eyes and bowed my head to them in thanks, then faced forward once more.

Hades' voice cut through the swell of emotions within me before they could carry me away. "Be on your guard," he said. "These readings . . . it's likely rebounded energy from Acheron, especially considering how evenly distributed the output is over the planet's surface, but it's strong enough—and strange enough—that we can't ignore the possibility of a synthetic source."

"Like what?" I asked.

"Some new form of Tsakali tech, perhaps," Hades said. "I cannot be more specific than that. Apologies, Cora. Just . . ." He paused, hesitating. "Remain vigilant."

His words of caution struck a chord. *Remain vigilant.* Not, *Don't go.* Not, *It's too dangerous.* Just, *Remain vigilant,* without a hint of doubt in my ability to see the mission through.

It was impossible for my thoughts not to venture into disturbing territory and to imagine what Raiden would have said. *You're not going. I won't let you. Don't do this.*

My nails dug into my thighs, and I clenched my jaw, Raiden's imagined words cutting deep.

You don't need to do this, Cora. Just let me go.

I turned my face away from Selene as I battled Raiden's ghost. He hadn't given me any say in his grand sacrifice. So he didn't get to have any say in my comparably far less doomed mission to rescue him.

I jutted my lower jaw forward, willing my chin not to tremble, and cleared my throat. I turned back to Selene. "Ready?"

"Ready."

5

F LAMES ENGULFED THE *ARGO* as we entered Othrys' atmosphere. It was eerily quiet within the ship, save for the creepy knocking sound on the outer hull that so often accompanied passage through a planet's atmosphere.

I gripped the fronts of my armrests, my shoulders tucked in against my neck, and my entire body tensed. These seventy seconds were the only ones our ship would be exposed and vulnerable, given away by the blaze surrounding the *Argo*, formed from shredded atoms.

Thankfully, the entire planet was covered in a thick layer of rust-colored clouds, camouflaging our fiery arrival, if not hiding it completely. If any cloaked ships were orbiting the planet *and* they noticed our fireball, they would hopefully assume we were nothing more than natural space matter passing through the atmosphere.

The inferno visible through the viewscreen gradually dissipated until the vibrant crimson flames faded, leaving only the dull carmine clouds. The tension tightening my shoulders eased, and I deliberately relaxed in my seat as I stared through the viewscreen, squinting in an attempt to pierce the dense cloud cover. Without feedback from the scouting drones, we had no clue what we would find down on the surface of the planet.

"Would you look at that?" Selene said, hitching her chin toward the chart displayed on the holoscreen hovering beside the navigation sphere. The curve of her lips warred with the shadows in her eyes.

A blinking red beacon had just appeared on the chart. I recognized the ship's numerical tag. The pirate shuttle. Raiden's ship. Renewed hope of finding him swept away all my doubts.

"We should get a visual of the surface *right . . . about . . . now,*" Selene said, drawing out those last three words.

As she spoke, the clouds thinned, revealing the ghostly outlines of dozens of tall, skeletal buildings shrouded in a thick, almost incandescent greenish fog. The air was further clouded by rust-tinged ashfall. The towering, decrepit structures reached so high that the tops of some disappeared into the crimson clouds. Most of the buildings appeared to have more than four sides. Even reduced to structural elements, it was clear that, long ago, this city had been far more advanced than those we had left behind on Earth.

"What city do you think this is?" I asked, awed by the unexpected view of this ancient metropolis. I wasn't sure why I even bothered to ask. My knowledge of the ancient Tsakali civilization was nonexistent.

"I have absolutely no idea," Selene said distractedly, leaning forward and squinting to peer through the clouded air. "There must be volcanic activity nearby," she murmured and swiped her fingers over the holoscreen.

The display on the broad viewscreen curving around the front of the ship's interior altered, neon-blue outlines of buildings overlaying our obscured view of the city.

"That's better," Selene muttered as she settled back in her seat.

As Selene steered the *Argo* around dilapidated towers, I alternated between looking out the viewscreen and checking the hovering navigation chart for the blinking beacon marking the location of Raiden's ship. Even without the fog, we would have been too far away to see the pirate shuttle, but knowing that didn't stop me from peering through the viewscreen, searching for the ship anyway.

Selene slowly guided the *Argo* lower, and soon we were skimming a couple dozen feet above street level. Or what would have been a street before it had been littered with chunks of fallen debris from the crumbling towers. Everything—the pitted and decaying facades of the buildings, the rubble clogging the streets, the ground itself—was tinted by the rusty red of dried blood from the falling ash.

I spotted a vein of neon green cut through the carmine stain on the exterior wall of a nearby tower as we passed by. I leaned forward, squinting as I peered through the fog and ash, focusing on the zigzagging streak of green. Was it *glowing*? As with the fog's strangely luminous quality, it was hard to tell in the ruby daylight.

I glanced at Selene sidelong.

"I saw it," she said without me even having to ask.

She swiped and tapped the holoscreen a few more times, activating the organic matter filter. A second layer overlaid the view of the fog-shrouded cityscape on the other side of the viewscreen. The crooked lines spider webbing over the sides of the skeletal buildings reminded me of veins blackened by poisoned blood.

"It's all over the place," Selene added.

I leaned forward further to peer down at the ground, and sure enough, there it was. "What is it?"

Selene frowned and shook her head. "Looks like some kind of fungus. We'll analyze a sample when we land."

She increased the intensity of the organic matter filter with a slide of her fingertip up the edge of the holoscreen. Tiny specs of white filled the viewscreen until we could barely see the ruins beyond.

"The air is clogged with spores, so we'll need to wear respirators." She angled her head to the side. "Probably would've had to anyway, based on the radiation levels. I can't imagine the air here being breathable for long."

Selene drew her fingertip back down the edge of the holoscreen, and the opaque cloud of spores faded to the semiopaque fog. I wondered if the spores were what gave the fog its eerie luminosity.

"I've seen something like this before," I told Selene, settling back in my seat. "In the labyrinths Hades built back on Earth. It had a psychotropic effect."

"Well, we'll know if this stuff is similar soon enough." Selene steered the *Argo* to the right, flying around a hexagonal skyscraper that pierced the cloud cover. "Raiden's ship should be just around this tower."

I glanced at the navigation chart, noting how much closer the beacon from the pirate shuttle was now than it had been the last time I had looked. My heart thudded in my chest, suddenly beating double-time. I nodded my acknowledgment of Selene's words but didn't trust my voice enough to speak. In a matter of minutes, I would likely have the answers I needed. We would either find Raiden alive . . .

Or we wouldn't.

As Selene guided the *Argo* around the last corner of the tower, a crater came into view up ahead, at least a hundred yards in diameter and surrounded by demolished buildings. My heart turned leaden and sank into my stomach. Had Raiden's ship caused this crater? It was hardly larger than the *Argo*. *Could* a ship of that size cause this kind of damage?

But then I noticed the thick layer of ash and glowing green veins of fungus covering the lip of the crater. Either the fungus spread incredibly fast, or something else had caused this crater a long time ago.

As we floated across the threshold of the crater, I spotted the wreckage of a ship through the fog near the far side of the enormous depression. The closer we drew, the clearer the crash site became. The damage was bad enough that I wouldn't have been able to recognize the ship as the pirate shuttle without the beacon for confirmation, but it hadn't been completely obliterated. A long trench had been gouged into the ground, marking its crash path.

My estimation of Raiden's survival odds plummeted as we closed in on the wrecked ship. I was having a hard time imagining anyone living through such a crash landing. Selene's sidelong glances my way were palpable, but I couldn't tear my focus away from the impact site. I couldn't stop searching for *him*. Or rather, for *his body*.

As soon as the *Argo* touched down, I unfastened my seat restraints and ran toward the back of the cabin. My heart drummed a primal beat in my chest, urging me forward.

"Cora, wait!" Selene called.

My hand stalled mere inches from punching the button to lower the rear loading ramp. I glanced back at Selene over my shoulder. Meg and the others were on their feet and heading my way.

Selene crouched near the center of the ship and yanked open the door to a storage hatch in the floor. She reached into the recess and pulled out a long steel box. She flipped the lid open, revealing a neatly packed row of low-profile respirators, then started pulling out masks and tossing them to the Amazons nearest her.

I hurried back toward Selene and caught the mask she lobbed my way. I fit the breathing apparatus over the lower half of my face, then awkwardly secured the strap around the back of my head without lowering my hood. With my respirator in place, I rushed back to the control pad on the wall at the back of the cabin and turned to watch the others, waiting until everyone had their masks in place. When everyone was ready, I punched the button to lower the ramp.

It seemed to take forever, giving the dread in my gut plenty of time to tie itself into double and triple knots. Once the ramp touched the ground, I ran down and sprinted across the ash-covered crater floor toward the wreckage, squinting against the ash flakes sticking to my lashes. The ground was oddly cushioned beneath my feet, making my steps springier.

Pieces of the pirate shuttle's exterior littered its crash path, scattered like breadcrumbs. The closer I drew, the more certain I became of Raiden's demise. Nobody could survive such a crash, especially not without armor. The last vestiges of my hope grasped at straws, filling my mind with fanciful ideas about Raiden finding some high-tech armor or a mech suit on the pirate shuttle and donning it before the crash.

My steps slowed, instinct wanting to put some distance between myself and whatever I would find inside what remained of the crashed ship. Bile rose up my throat as I anticipated the inevitable.

Hesitantly, I approached the open side hatch, having passed the door itself a ways back. The front third of the ship wasn't in terrible shape, which was promising, considering that's where Raiden would have been while piloting it. I stood just outside the threshold amid the falling ash and stared into the cabin. Cables and panels hung down from the ceiling, sparking intermittently, and iridescent fungus spores glowed in the dim interior.

Footsteps shushed through the ash behind me. "Do you want me to go in first?" Selene asked, stopping beside me.

I closed my eyes, took a deep breath, then opened them and shook my head.

"Do you want to go in alone?"

Clenching my jaw, I nodded. And then I reached for the edge of the open hatch, lifted my foot, and hoisted myself up and into the ship.

I stood just inside the wreckage and scanned the cabin. The dislodged pilot's seat. The shattered viewscreen. The missing back right quadrant of the ship. But among all the destruction, there was no body. No Raiden.

The only hint that anyone had been present during the crash was a smear of blood on the floor near the base of the pilot's seat, beneath the crushed navigation sphere.

I quickly walked the inside perimeter of the cabin, my focus constantly moving. Searching. Hunting.

Raiden wasn't here.

But he had been. I glanced at that lone smear of blood again. And he had been injured.

Either someone else had moved him, or he hadn't just survived the crash; he had been in good enough shape to walk away from it.

Dazedly, I made my way back to the open hatch and jumped down to the cushy crater floor. I suddenly felt energized with hope. It thrummed through me.

"Well?" Selene asked, one of her laser pistols in hand but lowered to the ground. She stepped closer to me, her stare searching mine. "Is he in there?"

I shook my head as I scanned the women standing watch around the wreckage, then my focus shifted past them to the ruined city shrouded in fog. I fought the urge to raise my hands to my hood and push it back, enabling my psychic radar to search for Raiden. If he really was alive, psychically searching would be so much faster and easier than tracking him the old-fashioned way.

"He's out there, somewhere!" I said, my voice raised and urgent. "We need to look for tracks—"

Selene grabbed my arm, her grip firm enough to draw my attention back to her. She released me and forcefully touched her extended index finger to the front of her respirator, her brows bunched together, hinting at a concealed frown. She was telling me to control my volume. Shouting an order like that had been reckless.

"Sorry," I said, my voice hushed. "I wasn't thinking." At least not about *our* safety.

I was too busy wondering how I would ever be able to walk away from this place if we couldn't find him. If Raiden's trail ended here, I would never know what had happened to him. I would always wonder if I could have done more. If staying and searching another day, another hour, another five minutes would have made the difference. Where my sanity was concerned, it would have been better to find a body.

I shoved away the malignant thought as soon as it crossed my mind.

Selene touched her comms patch. "The mission is now search and rescue," she said, speaking to the entire team.

Selene reached into a pouch attached to her weapons belt and withdrew seven silver balls the size of a shooter marble. Scouting drones. She tossed them into the air, and they all sprouted wings and hovered a few feet overhead. She tapped her holoband a few times, and they vanished from sight.

"We'll break into three teams, each with an emergency kit," she said. "Between us and the drones, we'll find him." She scanned the others as they approached. "Comms still work locally, so stay on the group channel, and remember to only use your gifts as a last resort." Selene turned a hard stare on me. "And whatever you do, absolutely *do not* remove your hood to search for Raiden psychically. We will find him, but not at the expense of our own lives."

I nodded once, letting Selene know I had heard her, loud and clear.

6

M Y STOMACH TWISTED AS mild queasiness set in. For over an hour, we had been searching the ruins of the groaning buildings, slowly fanning out from the crater, and I wasn't sure if the nausea was a product of my nerves or if my body was beginning to show signs of radiation poisoning. Meg felt it too, so I leaned toward radiation poisoning being the cause.

It was more of an annoyance than anything truly worrisome—for *us*—the asclypos would fix us up good as new. My holoband assured me it would take over 24 hours to absorb enough radiation to kill me. Raiden was another matter entirely.

How long had he been here, out in the open without even a respirator to clean his air? How far along was his radiation poisoning? How lost was he to fungus-induced madness? It was impossible not to imagine him deranged, with glowing green irises like those of the family we had found in the labyrinth in Brazil. And what about his other injuries? There had been blood at the crash site.

I feared if we didn't find him soon, it wouldn't matter if we found him at all. And that was assuming he was still alive. Depending on the seriousness of his injury and how much blood he was losing, he could have perished shortly after fleeing the wreckage.

I paused at the deep, hair-raising groan from the tower to my right, one of the skyscrapers that vanished into the crimson cloud cover. The buildings had been making such unsettling sounds the entire time we had been searching the city. Setting me further on edge, I could *feel* the fungus beneath my boots. It pulsed with energy, just like the fungus in the labyrinth.

I lowered my laser pistol and glanced around at my companions, Caly and Melyse, who scoured opposite sides of the rubble-strewn street for signs of someone passing through recently while I searched the central stretch of the road. The rust-colored ash that coated everything in this place, paired with the gusting wind, made tracking Raiden nearly impossible. Whatever tracks he may have left behind were likely covered with fresh ashfall or had been blown away, which meant we had to focus on less impermanent signs that he had been through here. Namely, blood. But that, too, was hard to see against the red ash.

Our luck finding resources had been better, though we weren't really even looking at this point. Selene's team had already found and flagged a location with an ample supply of flerovium, and Meg's team stumbled across ancient, deteriorated curium cartridges. The cartridges themselves were useless, but it wasn't like the curium stored within could have spoiled over thousands—or even tens of thousands—of years.

But no sign of Raiden yet, beyond the crash site itself.

I raised one hand, touching the rim of my protective hood. I could slip it back, just for a second, and see if I sensed any other minds nearby.

Then, we would at least know if we should move on from this part of the city to search another.

Caly crouched near the remains of what I suspected had once been a vehicle—or an exceptionally large chunk of the skyscraper—and I held my breath. Had she found something? But she quickly stood and moved on.

Could I do it? Could I risk her life—all their lives, as well as my own—if it fast-tracked the search for Raiden?

Hadn't I already?

"Cora!" Meg's voice hissed through my mind. She must have picked up on my rising frustration and sensed I was considering doing something extremely foolish.

I let my hand drop. "I'm not going to do it," I told her through our bond.

"I appreciate that," Meg said, her projected voice dry. "But that's not it." Her next words were spoken aloud and delivered through our group comms link. "I found something. Fresh blood."

Only then did I notice the niggling thrill of excitement that wasn't my own. I closed my eyes, focusing on the intangible cord connecting us, and slipped deeper into Meg's mind until her senses became my own and I saw the world through her eyes.

A bloody handprint smeared over the subtly glowing fungus blanketing a door frame. No blood on the ground, which made me think this was from a gut wound and Raiden was applying pressure to the injury. Thus, the bloodied hand.

Meg swabbed a sample and fed it into her holoband. I watched the small screen projected above her forearm as it analyzed the blood. The holoscreen flashed red, then flickered to green and back to red, like it was having a hard time reading the sample.

Finally, it settled on green. The blood was a match for Raiden.

Adrenaline surged within me, making my entire body thrum with the anticipation of victory. We found him.

"Follow the trail," I told her silently. "I'm on my way."

I pulled out of Meg's mind and raised my eyelids, briefly disoriented by the change in perspectives. Caly and Melyse stood nearby, awaiting direction.

I glanced at Melyse, then focused on Caly. "Meg analyzed a sample. It's Raiden's blood," I told them. "Come on." I turned partway and started toward Meg's portion of the ruined city, following our invisible bond like it was the glowing guide trail in a video game.

We raced up five blocks, then took a left and followed that street until we reached the tower marked by Raiden's bloody handprint. Meg was deep within the building, still on the ground floor but in some area with little light save for that given off by the veins of luminescent fungus crisscrossing every visible surface and the incandescent spores clouding the air. Raiden must have been out of his mind to the fungus madness to have sought refuge here.

"Stay out here and keep watch," I told Caly and Melyse. "When Selene arrives, send her in."

They nodded, and Caly unslung the strap of our team's emergency kit from her shoulder, handing it to me. I hoisted it over my head, securing the long strap across my body, then hurried into the building, feeling my way toward Meg. I found her in an inner room, following a solid line of blood smeared along one wall to where it disappeared through a doorway, the way partially blocked by a door hanging on decomposing hinges. The opening glowed a haunting yellow-green, as though the space beyond was even more infested with the fungus.

I crossed the room, heading straight for the doorway. Meg halted her approach and raised her laser pistol, nodding to let me know she had my back. I reached out with one hand, my own laser pistol angled down at the floor. If Raiden was in there and out of his mind enough to attack me, the last thing I wanted was to accidentally shoot him.

The door refused to open further, so I slipped through the existing gap. I entered a small room with walls, ceiling, and floor so densely coated in the glowing fungus that it was impossible to see individual veins and instead appeared to be a solid mass. A haze of glowing spores filled the air like a toxic glitter bomb.

"Raiden!" I hissed his name as I rushed forward.

He lay sprawled facedown on the floor in the middle of the room, looking like he had collapsed mid-step. His boots had cut a visible trail through the inches-thick carpet of neon-green fungus. I could only imagine the state of mind that had driven him to seek refuge in here. My stomach knotted, and I rubbed my chest with one hand, my heart physically aching. He must have been so afraid, all alone in this hellish place.

"I'm here, Raiden," I said as I dropped to my knees beside him.

A cloud of incandescent spores exploded from the floor, momentarily shrouding us both. I waved my arms in a useless attempt to clear the air, then reached forward and gripped Raiden's shoulder. Grunting, I rolled him onto his back. The patch of squashed fungus where he had lain was stained with blood. The source was impossible to miss. The lower half of the front of Raiden's gray t-shirt was soaked through with blood.

Gently, I lifted the hem of his shirt to see the wound. The fabric peeled away reluctantly, making me wince. From the looks of it, Raiden had been impaled by something during the crash. But that wasn't what made my blood run cold.

I swallowed roughly as I stared at the neon veins shooting out from the swollen, seeping wound. Raiden wasn't just injured. The fungus had infected him, exactly as I had feared.

Again, I thought back to the fungus-infected family in the labyrinth. It had turned them rabid, taking over their minds and controlling their bodies. I could only imagine what it was doing to Raiden right now. If he was even still alive.

I found his wrist and pressed my fingers to his pulse point. The thrum of life was thready, but it was there. He wasn't dead yet. Which meant I could still save him.

"We have to get him back to the ship," I told Meg over my shoulder as I shifted the emergency bag onto my lap.

"We can't carry him on our own," Meg said, her voice audible to my ears and through the comms patch. "We need a field stretcher." A real, physical one, since we couldn't risk making a stretcher from psychic energy at the moment.

I yanked the zipper on the emergency bag open and dug around until I found a clotting bandage. I tore the package open, tossed the wrapper aside, and carefully covered the oozing, infected wound on Raiden's abdomen.

Selene strode past Meg, entering the fungus-infested room. "The asclypos on the *Argo* isn't working." She kneeled on the opposite side of Raiden, facing me.

"Which is why we need to get him back to the *Elysium.*"

Tentatively, Selene shook her head and hesitated before saying, "Honestly, Cora, I'm not sure we should."

Taken aback, I jerked my head up and speared her with a hard stare.

"Just hear me out," Selene said, raising her hands defensively. "We don't know what the fungus will do once we bring it on board the ship. What if it spreads like it has down here?" She raised her eyebrows, her stare imploring me to see past my Raiden-shaped blind spot. To truly hear her. To understand. "We have his consciousness orb." She glanced down at Raiden, just for a moment. "There's a good chance this body won't even survive the trip back to the *Argo*, let alone to the *Elysium*." Compassion softened her eyes. "Maybe it's time to cut our losses and give him a fresh start in the simulation."

"But—but—" Slowly, I shook my head, returning my stare to Raiden's unconscious form. He appeared half dead already. More than.

"We don't know how long he's been here," Selene said. "We have no idea how much radiation he's soaked up—or how deep the fungal infection goes."

I heard others enter the room, but I couldn't tear my stare away from Raiden. How was I supposed to explain to her that *this body* mattered to me when, for millennia, the physical form had been little more than a disposable vessel to Olympians?

Again, I shook my head. "I can't—" My stare locked with Selene's. "I'll take him—just me on the *Argo* while you guys continue the search for the elements down here." The words tumbled out of me in a rush. "Once I'm within range of the *Elysium*, I'll speak with Hades. I'll explain the situation. If he shares your concerns and denies us the right to board, that will be the end of it."

But deep down, I knew he would never deny me. Besides, if this fungus really was the same as what he had used in the labyrinths, I didn't think he would turn us away, as he clearly knew how to handle it.

The crease that formed between Selene's brows suggested she suspected the same thing. Hades would let me board, no matter what.

Selene held my stare for a long, tense moment. Finally, she nodded, and her focus shifted past me. She waved the others forward, then stood, making way for Caly and Kyra to lay out a field stretcher alongside Raiden. Selene and Melyse gripped Raiden's shoulders while Meg and Helyna grasped his knees and calves.

"On three," Selene said. "One. Two. Three."

With a chorus of grunts, the four women lifted Raiden a few inches off the ground, holding him just long enough for Caly and Kyra to slide the stretcher underneath him. I manned one of the side handles while we hauled him back to the ship, feeling too much like a pallbearer for my liking. Every other step, I glanced down at Raiden, fearing he was already too far gone even for the asclypos to fix.

When we reached the *Argo*, we loaded Raiden onto the ship and strapped him into the rightmost pilot seat. I double-checked that all his safety restraints were snug, then straightened and sidestepped to the other pilot seat. I dropped into the chair and strapped myself in. As I tightened the restraints, I glanced up at Selene, who stood with her hip leaned against the front control console. Her arms were crossed over her chest, and her assessing stare was fixed on Raiden.

"I'll return as quickly as possible," I told Selene.

She would continue the search for resources to refill the element cartridges with the rest of the team while I ferried Raiden back to the *Elysium*. Once he was safely on board the ark ship, I would fly the *Argo* back down to Othrys to either rejoin Selene and the others or to retrieve them, depending on Hades' assessment of the radiation poisoning situation.

Selene nodded, but her focus didn't stray from Raiden.

"Selene," I said, going still, my voice harder than I had intended. "Are we going to have a problem?"

Selene looked at me, her eyes the only part of her body that shifted. She stared at me for a long moment, glanced at Raiden once more, then returned her focus to me. "No," she said, relaxing her arms. "No problem." Despite her show of standing down, her stare remained steady, challenging. "I trust you to make the right call. You won't endanger the others. You won't endanger your mom."

I gulped. I hadn't considered that. My mom. The others. Hades.

I had only been thinking about Raiden. About preserving his chance at life. About proving that I really did deserve his love. That I really did love him.

Selene pushed off from the control console and stepped around Raiden's seat. She paused, resting her hand on the top of his seatback. "This doesn't feel right," she said, her voice a low murmur, muffled further by her respirator. "After a crash like that, he should be in worse shape than this."

I laughed bitterly. "He's barely breathing," I said. "How much worse shape could he be in?"

Selene gave me a pointed stare. Dead. He could be dead. He *should* be dead. The unspoken words hung between us, clogging the air in the ship's cabin. Unease took root in my belly, mingling with mild nausea caused by the radiation.

"Have a safe trip," Selene said. And then she turned and strode away.

7

R AIDEN LET OUT A groan just as we broke free from the planet's dragging atmosphere and entered the frictionless vacuum of
space. The *Argo* sped up as the gravitational pull lessened, and I hastily set
a course for the *Elysium*, cloaked but detectable to friendly ships already
registered on its network.

Once we were en route, I pulled my respirator down to hang looped
around my neck, unfastened my seat restraints, and slid over the edge of
my seat to kneel beside Raiden's. I was exposing myself to the fungus,
but our flight path was programmed into the ship, and it seemed worth
it to let him see my face. To let him know he wasn't alone anymore.

"Hey," I said, reaching for his hand. "I'm here." I clasped it between
both of mine and gave a reassuring squeeze. "I'm here, Raiden."

My heart skipped a beat as his lashes fluttered. He blinked his eyes
open, and my heart full-on stumbled.

"Hey." My lips curved into a trembling smile, and tears spilled over
the brims of my eyelids, streaming down my cheeks. "You're going to
be okay," I told him, figuring this was one of those situations where

motivation mattered more than truth. Believing he was going to survive might just be the thing that saved him.

Raiden focused on me, his brow furrowing. There was no recognition in his stare. There was only confusion. And was that a hint of green in his brown irises, or was my mind playing tricks on me? Was it possible for the fungus to infect his brain that quickly?

I pushed my hood back, figuring we were far enough away from Othrys to no longer need the protection of the orichalcum-laced fabric. Besides, Raiden's mind had been unguarded down on the planet, and he hadn't been swarmed by unfriendlies—Titan or otherwise. He had been utterly alone.

I sensed his mind, the familiar structure of his neural pathways, but the pattern of his active consciousness felt strange—remote and somehow muted. He had no surface thoughts. Absolutely none. I focused on him, delving deeper into his mind, but I found no discernible thoughts at all. No emotions. No memories. Nothing beyond the vague, structural sense of *him*.

I had never felt anything like it before. Had the fungus done this to him? Was it suppressing his conscious self? Or had something else happened? Perhaps a head injury sustained during the crash? Or a mental break?

I peered up at Raiden, into his vacant stare, searching for some hint of recognition or even of awareness. "What happened to you?" I whispered.

Raiden blinked, the movement slow and catlike. I sensed some activity in his mind, but it was too faint—too muted—to discern. His silence stretched on, and he continued to stare at me like we hadn't grown up together. Like he had never seen me before in his life. Unease sent cracks through the giddiness I felt at finding him alive.

Selene had been correct. This didn't feel right. *He* didn't feel right.

I wished Meg were with me. She had an innate grasp of the physiological workings of the brain. I was certain she would have had a much clearer understanding of whether this was the influence of the fungus or if he might have suffered some other sort of trauma. She would at least have had *some idea* of what was going on in his head. Or, in his case, what *wasn't* going on.

"Do you want me to merge with you?" Meg offered, her voice streaming into my mind through our bond. I had the vague sense of her gazing up into the cavernous rafters of a groaning building.

"No," I said, shaking my head even as I continued to search Raiden's blank stare. "Focus on what you're doing down there. We'll be back on the *Elysium* soon enough."

Meg sent me a long-distance hug, letting me know she was ready to help if I changed my mind, then withdrew.

Sighing, I glanced at the navigation chart and stood. "Sit tight," I said, placing Raiden's hand on his thigh before sidestepping back to my seat. "We're almost there." I sat and secured my safety restraints, shooting furtive glances at Raiden out of the corner of my eye every few seconds.

His expression remained vacuous. Not merely unreadable, but empty. Just like his mind.

"Cora?" It was Hades, his voice choppy through the comms patch. "Can . . . hear me?"

I touched my comms patch. "I can hear you, but not clearly," I responded.

"It's the interference from Acheron," Hades said, the feed no longer cutting out. "I've been hailing you for a few minutes."

I frowned, sending another worried glance at Raiden. His blank stare was more than a little unsettling, so I returned my focus to the navigation chart.

"I found him," I told Hades. "Raiden. He's with me now, but . . ." I licked my lips, finding it unnerving to be talking about Raiden to Hades while Raiden was sitting beside me, staring at me. I angled my face away from Raiden and lowered my voice, hoping he couldn't hear my next words. "Something's *wrong.*"

"He's injured?" Hades asked.

"No—yes," I said, shaking my head. "He is—pretty badly—but it's not that." I paused, considering how to explain the fungus situation. "You know the fungus you used in the labyrinths?"

"Pasitheorales Viride. Of course," Hades said.

"Well, it was down there, on Othrys," I told him. "Or, at least, I think it was the same stuff. We took a sample." I activated my holoband, and after a few taps and swipes, sent the readings to Hades. "I just sent you the data."

"Received." He was quiet for a moment. "Yes, this is a variation of the same strain of Pasitheorales Viride," he said. "Astute observation."

I nodded to myself and again angled my face away from Raiden. "It seems to have infected him," I explained in a hushed voice. "Is it safe to bring him onto the *Elysium*?"

"With precautions," Hades said. "We'll hold the *Argo* in a quarantine bubble until it can be decontaminated. No point in doing that until you fly back and retrieve the others. We'll do the same with Raiden and anyone who assists in his recovery until they, too, can be decontaminated."

"Okay, good," I said, nodding more enthusiastically. Hades had a plan—a logical plan that didn't sound remotely far-fetched. He wasn't reaching just to please me. I cleared my throat, the queasiness lessening slightly. "Thanks, Hades," I said, unable to hide the tremor in my voice.

"For you, anything," he said resolutely.

His words and the sincerity with which they had been delivered caught me off guard. My nostrils flared and my eyes filled with a second wave of tears. I jutted my jaw forward, determined to maintain my composure this close to boarding the *Elysium*.

"The external airlock door is open," Hades informed me. "I'll see you momentarily."

"Thanks," I repeated, touching my comms patch to mute the connection. I glanced at Raiden and forced a smile. "We'll be there soon. We'll get you all patched up and—" I swallowed the words *back to normal*. "And everything will be okay." I flashed him another, shakier smile before whispering, "I'm so glad we found you."

I almost told him I should have gone with him. That he should have let me. But in his current, dazed state, rehashing what had happened in the transport hangar would be a one-sided conversation.

I refocused on the navigation chart, and the viewscreen behind it, waiting for the moment when we passed through the stealth shields and the *Elysium* became visible. The viewscreen flickered suddenly. And then, there was the behemoth ark ship in all her glory.

I settled my hands on the navigation sphere and took manual control of the *Argo*, altering our trajectory to aim for the waiting airlock. As I guided the smaller ship, I felt equal parts hyper-focused and dazed, like I was in a dream. The exterior door slid shut behind the stern of the *Argo*, and then the inner airlock door glided open, revealing the cavernous transport hangar. A shimmering silver energy film blocked the opening.

The quarantine bubble Hades had promised. Beyond it, Hades waited with my mom and Emi. Sharay, one of the new Amazons, was there, too.

As I rolled the navigation sphere forward, the *Argo* inched ahead. The silver energy barrier molded to the front of the ship. I waited until we had cleared the inner airlock door by a few yards, leaving enough room to lower the rear ramp but not wanting to overstretch the quarantine bubble, then set the *Argo* down.

Hastily, I unfastened my seat restraints. "I'll be right back," I told Raiden as I stood, hesitating only for a moment before hurrying to the rear of the ship.

I smacked my palm against the button to lower the ramp, and it opened just in time for me to watch the airlock seal shut behind us. I glanced over my shoulder at Raiden while I waited for the ramp to finish lowering. He remained in his seat, restrained by the safety belts, his neck craned to watch me. I hadn't noticed him blink this whole time.

Once the ramp touched the floor of the hangar, I hurried down it and toward the small group waiting on the other side of the energy barrier. Sharay already had a stretcher of ruby-red psychic energy formed and waiting for Raiden. Another silver energy barrier surrounded each of them like a second skin—except for Sharay, who was coated in glittering red psychic energy from head to toe. These were individual quarantine bubbles originating from the hockey puck-sized devices affixed to their chests.

Emi's expression was wrought with hope and fear, making my heart lurch. I had brought her son back, but to what end? He was alive, but even now, I wasn't sure we could save him.

"He's in there," I told them, twisting my upper body to glance behind me into the ship. "He's conscious, but he seems . . ." I struggled with how to describe Raiden's current state of mind. "In shock."

Emi pressed her lips together, a mask of sheer determination settling over her face. She exchanged a glance with Sharay, and the two of them stepped forward, pushing through the shimmering white film of the larger quarantine bubble that surrounded the *Argo*.

I watched them climb up the ramp and disappear into the *Argo*, then turned my attention back to Hades and my mom.

Hades held out his hand, an unused quarantine generator resting on his palm. He raised his eyebrows.

I could have surrounded myself in a protective bubble of psychic energy, just like Sharay had done, but I figured it was probably smartest to conserve my psychic energy for when I rejoined the team on Othrys.

"Thanks," I said, reaching out to take it as I stepped closer to the energy barrier separating us.

I affixed the quarantine generator to my chest, off to one side to avoid my regulator. I pressed the button in the center of the circular device, and a shimmering silver energy barrier spread out from it to encase me completely. There was a momentary sense of static electricity, like when passing through a holographic barrier, that caused the hairs all over my body to stand on end.

I stepped forward, pushing through the shimmering barrier of the larger quarantine bubble. I held up a hand when my mom moved to greet me, her arms raising for a hug. "We have to stay in our own bubbles," I explained. "If our barriers touch, they could merge, and any contaminants can pass through."

"Oh," my mom said, lowering her arms and stepping back. "I didn't realize."

I flashed her a weak smile.

"You must be so relieved," she said, her gaze scouring my face like she was searching for evidence of the emotion.

At the sound of boots clanging on the metal floor behind me, I turned to watch Emi and Sharay make their way down the ramp, the stretcher carrying Raiden contained within his own quarantine bubble hovering between them. Emi's eyes met mine as she passed. She smiled, but I could sense the crippling anxiety masked beneath the expression. She understood now what I had meant about Raiden seeming *in shock*, and she was as unsettled by it as I had been.

I watched them hurry away with Raiden, then turned back to Hades and my mom. "He seems to have some kind of amnesia," I told them. "He crashed in the middle of some ruins—a huge city—but survived, obviously. He was injured in the crash. We found blood on the ship, but he was able to walk away. He must have been disoriented because he wandered pretty far. We found him in a room in one of the ruined buildings."

My mom covered her mouth with one hand as I spoke.

I focused all my attention on Hades. "It was filled with the fungus—the Viride stuff. The air was completely saturated with glowing spores, and it has definitely infected his wound. Do you think it could already have taken over his mind? Is that why he feels—I don't know—*hollow*?"

Hades frowned thoughtfully. "It is possible, but I cannot say without further information. Once Emi has run a full diagnostic on him in the asclypos, we'll have a clearer idea of what's going on with him."

I nodded to myself. I had been expecting Hades to say something like that. He was always data first, conclusions later.

"At least we found him." I looked from Hades to my mom, letting myself feel some of that relief she had been searching for. "The hardest part is over."

8

"So, we have two options now that we have recovered Raiden," Hades said, striding along beside me down the broad main corridor of the *Elysium*.

We were on our way to the Med Sector, walking together but careful to keep enough distance between us to prevent our quarantine bubbles from merging. If, somehow, this variation of the fungus was more invasive and damaging than the version Hades had used in the labyrinths, I absolutely could not risk infecting Hades with it. More than anyone else—more than Raiden or my mom or all our psychic warriors combined, myself included—Hades *had* to endure. He was the best hope of survival for both Olympians and humankind. Without him, the *Elysium* would never reach Terra.

Touching was still a relatively new thing for me *with anyone*, but it was especially novel for Hades and me, having been forbidden by Demeter, the leader of the Order of Amazons, for pretty much all my lifetimes. But even so, I despised the sense of forced separation. The inability of our arms to brush together. Of the backs of our hands to touch. I had always been hyperaware of Hades' presence, of his physical space relative to mine. His nearness. Now, I was all too aware of his distance.

"We can either remain where we are and commit to searching Othrys for the resources we need to refill the depleted element cartridges," Hades went on. "Or we can leave after you've returned to the planet to retrieve the team."

We stopped at a double door panel marked *MED SECTOR* by a plaque above the doorway. The door panel whooshed open, and we continued on. Hades was waiting on an analysis from the radiation readings in the holoband's logs to set a more accurate departure timer for the team still down on the planet. We needed to get them out of there before the radiation poisoning reached lethal levels. But that meant I was stuck here, waiting on said analysis.

After all the weirdness with Raiden on the *Argo*, I figured my time was best spent checking on him before returning to Othrys. I wanted—needed—to make sure he would be all right, that I wouldn't fly back down to Othrys, only to return and find him gone. Dead. Uploaded.

"If we decide on the latter," Hades continued, "you must return to the planet to retrieve the remainder of your team immediately, so we can be on our way. Lingering here wastes valuable resources we have in extremely short supply."

I glanced at Hades, my eyebrows rising. "It's that bad?"

Hades nodded once.

I sighed and shook my head. "It's always something," I muttered.

Dread doused the last remaining spark of relief from finding Raiden. He wasn't the only one facing a dire situation. We all were.

Sighing, Hades combed his fingers through his hair, the shoulder-length silver-blond strands unusually unkempt. How long had it been since he allowed himself any rest beyond the briefest possible session in an asclypos? Meg had assured me he wasn't bleeding inside his brain, but concern for his well-being tangled with the tightening knot in my belly.

"We were expecting this," Hades said.

"*We* were?" I asked, my voice heavy with skepticism.

"This ship's resources were vastly depleted when we found it," Hades said, nonplussed by my tone.

"I thought we refilled everything possible before leaving Earth," I said as we rounded a corner.

We entered a corridor lined with nearly two dozen evenly spaced doorways, each of which led to an asclypos chamber. All save for one near the end were open, suggesting they had entered the Med Sector by the opposite door. Raiden was in there, being assessed by the machine.

"We did," Hades said, shooting me a sidelong glance. "But some of the elements this ship requires to run aren't readily available in Earth's solar system, and we didn't have the time or resources to hunt elsewhere while preparing for the upload."

I snorted a derisive laugh. I knew I was poking at Hades, hanging on to this discussion with tooth and nail to keep my mind off the situation in the asclypos chamber at the end of the corridor.

Hades sighed dramatically. "Fine, Cora, *I* was expecting this."

The corners of my mouth tensed, lifting in the tiniest of smug smiles.

"*If* we can fully replenish all the element cartridges," Hades said, barreling onward, "we will be able to complete the trip to Terra without having to make another resource stop."

I chewed on the inside of my cheek as I considered the two options.

We could stay and search the fungus-infested planet, which could very well be hiding even deadlier dangers than those we currently knew about. It *was* the original Tsakali home world, after all. Of course, that same fact meant it might be the richest source of some of the rarer raw materials we needed to refill the element cartridges. Those that only a civilization capable of extraplanetary space travel could amass.

Or we could move on to a safer planet, but pickings elsewhere would be far slimmer. Elsewhere, we would likely have to make do with *just enough* to get by, requiring we make another stop along the way. There was no guarantee that we would find another planet with such promising resources.

"Were there any signs of recent occupation down there?" Hades asked, drawing my attention back to him. "Any hint at all that there might be Titans or other Tsakali?"

I shook my head. "It was just ruins and ash and that fungus," I told him. "The stuff is *everywhere*."

"Hm," Hades murmured, nodding thoughtfully. "It can be quite prolific in the right conditions."

I laughed quietly. "Yeah, well. Apparently, the surface of Othrys offers the *right conditions*."

A crease formed between Hades' brows. I had activated my regulator shortly after boarding the ship, suppressing my psychic gifts, but I didn't need my abilities to sense that the presence of the fungus troubled Hades more than he was letting on.

I frowned, narrowing my eyelids as I studied Hades' features. "What is it?"

His jaw tightened, and the skin around his eyes tensed. "The Pasitheorales Viride . . ." He took a deep breath, holding it for a few seconds before slowly releasing the air. "It's likely just a remnant from before the Tsakali abandoned Othrys, but . . ." His words trailed off as he released another sigh and raised a hand to rub the back of his neck. "*We* created the fungus," he finally said, his tone making it sound like a confession.

"What?" I blurted. "*Why?*"

His features hardened, concealing his emotions behind the stony facade. "Back on Olympus, before the war drove us away from our home," he explained. "We created the fungus with the intent that it could serve as an external well of psychic energy for the Amazons, so they wouldn't have to wait on their internal supply to replenish naturally."

"Seriously?" I asked, my eyebrows raised as high as they would go.

Hades tilted his head to the side. "Unfortunately, we were never able to make the energy contained within the fungus accessible to Amazons."

I tensed the corners of my mouth, stopping when we reached the sealed door panel to the occupied asclypos chamber. The control pad beside the door was framed with a red, glowing light, indicating that the asclypos within was in use. The knot of tension and unease loosened within me as I stared at the control pad. If the asclypos was in use, then Raiden was still alive.

With an exhale of relief, I turned to face Hades. "I'm sensing a *but* coming."

"*But*," Hades said, "the Tsakali got ahold of the tech, and unlike *our* psychics, theirs *could* access the energy stored within the fungus."

A chill cascaded over me, giving rise to goose bumps. When Raiden and I were trapped within the second labyrinth in Brazil, I had destroyed the thick wall of fungus blocking our path by sucking the energy out of it. Not like an Amazon. Like a *Titan*.

What the hell did *that* mean? I was different from other Amazons. I knew that. Everyone knew it. I was an engineered person, created on board the *Tartarus* by Hades and his Genetec team during the trip from Olympus to Earth. All the other Amazons, both Olympian and Zari, had been given life through natural reproduction. My genetic code had been derived from a massive database of Olympian DNA, randomized and reformed to create a unique being: me.

Had some element of the Tsakali, of the *Titans*, eked its way into my genetic code? I may have been engineered, but I was still organic, whereas the Tsakali were synthetic beings. They no longer even *had* DNA.

My thoughts spiraled, and I wondered if I should mention it to Hades. The only other person who knew I could absorb the energy from the fungus was Raiden. I glanced at the sealed door panel ahead. I doubted he would be mentioning it to anyone. I supposed Meg knew, too, but she would never betray me.

I squeezed my hands into tight fists, then stretched out my fingers. What would Hades think if he found out that, where the fancy fungus was concerned, I was more like a Tsakali than an Olympian? What about Selene? What would she think? What about the Zari Amazons, who had suffered catastrophic losses at the hands of a single Titan who had killed their sisters by sucking the psychic energy out of them? Would they fear I might do the same? *Could* I do the same?

"Since the Tsakali are no longer organic beings," Hades pondered aloud, "they don't suffer from the same psychotropic side effects when exposed to the fungus. I suppose they could have purposely cultivated an overgrowth of the stuff here on Othrys."

I watched him closely. Thankfully, he was too preoccupied with his own train of thought to notice my momentary freakout. I shoved the panic into the back of my mind and focused on Hades' words.

The corners of his mouth turned down, and his eyelids narrowed. "Or it could have occurred naturally," he mused. "With the frequent massive bursts of radiation from Acheron, the surface would be unlivable now, even for the Tsakali, but they *could* survive underground. I certainly wouldn't discount the possibility that they stationed some Titans on the planet, what with the plentiful source of psychic energy from the fungus. Perhaps they even harvest it and ship it off-world."

"So, you still think there's a chance of sustained Tsakali occupation down there, despite us finding no evidence of recent activity?" I clarified.

Hades nodded slowly.

"Then we abandon Othrys and move on, right?"

Hades pressed his lips together and exhaled through his nose. "We've already found much of what we need," he said. "We won't come across a richer source than *Othrys*."

"I know," I said begrudgingly. "I know."

Sighing, I turned toward the door panel and tapped the control pad. The small, red-framed screen lit up, displaying a view of the chamber within. Raiden lay stretched out on the asclypos while Emi stood beside the machine, studying the readings on the control panel. Her back was to the camera, and she hugged her middle like she was trying to hold herself together.

My heart ached for her and everything she was going through. For Raiden and all *he* had gone through. My shoulders slumped, and I bowed my head, breathing through the swelling grief. What if Raiden was doomed to live out the rest of his life as the hollow shell that had flown back from Othrys with me? Maybe Selene had been right, and the kinder, more compassionate option was to let this physical body go and upload his backup to the *Elysium*.

"Cora?" Hades said, his voice softening around my name. He moved closer to my side and reached for me, pushing against the barrier of his own shimmering silver quarantine bubble until it was just shy of touching mine.

How was he capable of such sympathy for my concern over Raiden, the man who held the other half of my heart? I didn't feel deserving of such devotion.

I shut my eyes, attempting to block out Hades' face. But there he was on the backs of my eyelids, visible through the porthole on the pirate shuttle as though he had flown off in Raiden's place.

My emotions snarled. My thoughts twisted and tangled.

Why had Raiden put me in that chokehold? *Why* had he thrown me off the shuttle? *Why* had he flown away *without me*? I could have *helped*.

I should have been relieved to have Raiden back here, safely undergoing treatment in an asclypos. But instead, I was hurt and angry. So incredibly angry. Raiden was lying in there, possibly dying, and all I could think about was how this all would have turned out differently if we had worked as a team rather than him taking away my choice. Why hadn't he trusted me to help? Why hadn't he believed in me enough to *let* me?

My heartbeat sped up. My breaths came faster. An invisible vice tightened around my chest, and my stomach twisted. I gripped my throat, my chest rising and falling rapidly as I attempted—and failed—to catch my breath.

I heard a faint sizzle and felt a popping in my ears. A firm hand settled on my shoulder, then slid behind my neck. Another arm wrapped around my back, and suddenly I was pressed against a warm, hard body. Hades' body. He held me in a steady embrace, the fingers of one hand splayed over the back of my head, pressing my cheek against his shoulder.

"I know I'm not him," Hades murmured. "But I am here, Cora. Whatever you need, I am here."

I gripped the sides of his tunic, fighting the panic constricting around my chest. His scent was foreign and familiar. Ancient and new.

Shallow breaths gradually became deep lungfuls of air. Of him. The tension eased from my limbs, then from my back, until, finally, I relaxed against Hades.

I peeled my eyelids open, noting the shimmering silver energy barrier surrounding us both. When Hades touched me, he had merged our quarantine bubbles. He had exposed himself to any and every contaminant I carried.

"What have you done?" I whispered.

He had just risked everything—*everything*—to comfort me.

Hades' hand slid down the back of my neck, and I raised my head from his shoulder to peer up at his face. His jaw was set, his features locked in an expression of fierce defiance.

The control pad for the door to the asclypos chamber chimed. I craned my neck, peering around Hades' shoulder just as the frame switched from bright red to subtle blue. Hades' hold on me loosened, and I took a reluctant step back. With another sizzle and a pop, our quarantine bubbles separated again, but the damage had been done. Hades was contaminated.

The door panel glided open, and Emi rushed out, passing through the thin, shimmering barrier of the quarantine field that had been set up within the chamber, her features tense with worry. She paused just outside the asclypos chamber and touched the small shield generator affixed to the front of her shirt, activating her personal quarantine bubble. When she noticed us standing in the corridor, she jumped slightly, one hand clutching her chest, the other extended to fend off attackers.

I raised my hands in a silent apology. "How is he?"

Emi sucked in a breath like she was going to respond, but then her brows bunched together and she shook her head.

I took a step toward her, then stopped, mindful of our quarantine bubbles. "He's going to be okay, isn't he?" I asked, craning my neck to look around her to the man stretched out on the asclypos.

"I—" Emi's hand tightened to a fist, gripping the front of her tunic. "I think so, yes. His physical injuries are extensive but treatable." She peeked over her shoulder at Raiden, then stepped out into the corridor, letting the door panel slide shut. "The asclypos directed me to leave the room while it treated him for the fungal infection." She cleared her throat, her focus shifting from me to Hades, then to the corridor stretching out behind us. "Mild radioactivity exposure . . ."

Hades nodded his understanding.

I was desperate to reach out and pull Emi into my arms. For someone who had gone nearly her whole life without the reassurance of physical touch, it was quickly becoming a necessary part of my existence.

Emi touched the control pad beside the door, and the frame reverted to glowing red. "I should get him some fresh clothes," she said, sidestepping to the clear side of the corridor. "The asclypos requested that nobody enter the chamber until this round of treatment has concluded, and it advised he should be kept in quarantine until the fungal infection is eradicated."

Hades and I turned, watching Emi retreat down the corridor until she disappeared around a corner.

I glanced at Hades sidelong, my lips pressed together into a slight frown. "I should get back to the others," I said, reluctance bleeding into my voice. I didn't want to leave.

"I'll keep an eye on her," Hades promised. He glanced at the door to the asclypos chamber. "On both of them."

9

"WHATEVER YOU DECIDE, I will support your decision," Hades said as we entered the transport hangar. His voice echoed in the cavernous space.

I glanced at him sharply. His were the first words either of us had spoken since leaving the Med Sector. My mind was such a tangle of worries—about Raiden and Emi, about Hades exposing himself to the fungus, about the team down on Othrys—that I couldn't immediately puzzle out his meaning. Through my bond with Meg, I knew the team was all right for now. They were definitely feeling the effects of the radiation, but not so intensely that the symptoms interfered with their mission.

"What are you—" Brow furrowing, I replayed Hades' words. *Whatever you decide, I will support your decision.* I started to shake my head, but then it clicked. "You mean about staying here to search or looking elsewhere?"

Hades nodded once. "Based on our current element cartridge levels—and even if we collected the resources your team has already flagged down there," he explained, "I'm not comfortable putting anyone into cryosleep at this point. With our extremely low levels of Technetium, anyone entering cryosleep would risk ending up like Selene's team."

An image of the mummified remains of the other Amazons we had found in the failed cryopods flashed through my mind, and I winced. They had failed for another reason—an overextended power core—but the result in our case would be the same.

It was impossible not to imagine Emi and my mom in such a wasted condition. Or Raiden and Hades. Oddly enough, my mind's eye fixated on an image of Fiona, body desiccated within a cryopod, her orange hair as vibrant and shocking as ever. I shuddered and shook my head in an effort to rid myself of the ghastly visions.

"We definitely don't want that," I muttered.

"No, we don't," Hades agreed. "Which means our options are limited to a smaller area should we decide to seek a new location to source what we need to replenish the element cartridges."

"I see," I said, my voice tight.

We stopped near the edge of the shimmering silver energy barrier surrounding the *Argo*, once again falling silent. I was hesitant to step through, to put another layer of separation between us.

"While the likelihood of finding all we need is substantially higher here than anywhere else within our current sphere of reach, the danger is also not insubstantial," Hades said. "As you and your team are the ones taking on all the risk here, I will defer to you on this decision."

I groaned. "No pressure." A bitter laugh escaped me, and I eyed Hades sidelong. "Which would you choose?"

Hades let out a humorless chuckle and clasped his hands behind his back. He blinked, shifting his focus from me to the lowered ramp of the

Argo. He might as well have mimed zipping his lips for all I was going to get out of him.

I sighed and tilted my head back, staring up at the orichalcum-laced steel beams crisscrossing the ceiling high above. After a long moment, I lowered my focus to the interior airlock door, like I could see through it and all the way down to the surface of *Othrys* where my team currently scoured the ruined city for resources. They were already risking their lives down there. Already up to their elbows in the engineered fungus. Already committed to the mission *here.*

"Better the devil you know," I murmured. At Hades' curious expression, I realized he didn't understand my meaning because he had never heard the saying before. Funny, considering his mythical counterpart was so often misinterpreted by modern people as a variation of the devil. I cleared my throat and clarified, "Than the devil you don't know."

Understanding lit his eyes, and the corner of his mouth rose in a hint of a smile. "Ah, yes. I see." His expression turned thoughtful. "So, you wish to remain here?"

I returned to staring at the airlock door. "I think we should stay," I said, however reluctantly. "Yes, Raiden ending up here is *extremely* suspicious, but we haven't found any signs that anyone else has been here recently." I looked at Hades, searching his face for any sign of approval or disapproval.

He kept his expression carefully blank. Was he considering the possibility that this was still some elaborate trap? If so, where was the snare? We already had Raiden. If the Tsakali had stashed him on Othrys as a way to lure us to this hellish planet, why hadn't they already attacked?

"Othrys is as close to a sure thing as we'll find," I added, unsure if I was trying to convince Hades or myself. "We would be crazy to turn our noses up at this score, even with the high likelihood of a Titan presence. And if anything changes down there—if we notice anything suspicious—we can always reassess."

Hades turned his face toward me, his eyes searching mine. For seconds, we held each other's gazes, the silence stretching out between us like a cord tethering us together. Whatever we decided to do would likely be the deciding factor in the success or failure of our mission. Would we push our luck on this planet or venture into the wild unknown?

Finally, Hades lowered his chin in assent. "I agree." The words hung in the air, resonant beyond their faint echo.

For several heartbeats, we lingered in the quiet, pondering the ramifications of the decision we had just made.

"Well," I said, then cleared my throat. My focus drifted from Hades to the ramp leading up to the rear of the *Argo*. "I should . . ." I pointed toward the smaller ship with my chin.

Hades lifted his forearm, flicking his fingers to bring up the small holographic screen of his holoband. He studied the screen for a moment, then dismissed it.

"Set a timer for six hours from now," he told me. "If your team spends much longer down there, the radiation sickness will be more severe, requiring multiple sessions in an asclypos, a more intensive course of treatment, and a longer recovery time. Absolutely do not surpass thirteen hours from now. At that point, radiation poisoning will verge on lethal for Selene and the others." After a moment, his throat bobbed and he added, "*You* could last a couple of hours longer without risking death."

Nodding to Hades, I added, "Hopefully, we'll be able to find everything we need by then." The situation was odd and unsettling, and it would be best for everyone if we could take our treatments on the road rather than hunkering down in orbit around Othrys and waiting for a full recovery before returning to the planet's surface to continue the search.

I took a step toward the shimmering barrier surrounding the *Argo* but paused when my personal quarantine bubble was near enough to sizzle but not close enough to merge with the larger field of energy. I peered over my shoulder, looking back at Hades. Our gazes locked, and his jaw clenched.

Be careful, his intense stare seemed to say, but he didn't voice the sentiment. I doubted he ever would. I had been inside his head enough times to know that he feared those words on his tongue would convince me he didn't think I was capable of completing the task.

"See you soon," I said and offered him a small smile, just the slightest curve of my lips. And then I turned away from him and stepped through the shimmering silver barrier surrounding the *Argo*.

"Oh, and Cora," Hades said when I started up the ramp.

I paused and turned partway. Would he actually say it this time?

Hades stood at the very edge of the barrier, so close that his personal quarantine bubble sparked and popped. "While you're down there, please scan the crash site with your holoband."

My eyebrows rose. I hadn't expected *that*. "Sure. Why?"

Hades hesitated only for a moment before responding. "Examining a rendering of the wreckage may give us more clarity as to what happened to Raiden and his ship before the crash landing," Hades said, his expression carefully blank. "A better understanding of all that Raiden went through down there will allow us to treat his trauma more effectively up here." Hades raised one hand and touched his first two fingertips to his temple.

"You got it," I said with a nod. My gut told me that wasn't Hades' entire reason for this request, but it was enough for me.

Our gazes lingered for a moment longer, but then I turned and ascended the ramp. Once I was on board the *Argo*, I stopped and turned to the control panel on the wall. I pressed my palm against the button to raise the ramp, watching Hades until he was no longer visible beyond the rising slab of metal.

Moments before the rear hatch sealed shut, Hades' voice drifted to my ears, so quiet I almost second-guessed that I had heard it at all. His hushed words made my breath catch.

"Be careful."

10

As soon as I landed the *Argo* in the crater on Othrys, I scanned the crash site with my holoband's recorder, slowly walking first the perimeter of the wreckage and then what remained of the shuttle's interior. Once the data was stored safely in my holoband, I homed in on my bond with Meg, following the invisible tether as I tracked her through the ruined city, my steps hastened by the eerie groaning of the ancient skyscrapers.

I found Meg with her holoband arm extended, scanning the rubble tucked into the far corner of a wide-open single-story building with more holes than roof in the high ceiling overhead. Selene and Caly stood huddled together near the center of the space, both women studying the small holoscreen hovering above Selene's forearm.

As I headed for the nearer pair, I glanced up at the darkening red sky through a broad gap in the decrepit ceiling. The ash fall had let up, for now. The nearby volcanoes must have fallen quiet for the time being.

"It'll be night soon," I commented, my voice low.

Selene studied the sky, her eyes narrowing as though she were frowning under her mask. She hadn't noticed *Acheron* was making its descent beyond the horizon. "I think we're almost done here anyway," she said, glancing at me, then back down at the holoscreen.

My eyebrows hitched upward, and I focused on my bond with Meg, skimming her mind for a progress update on the mission. I learned that the rest of the team was packing up the tagged resources and transferring them back to the crater while Meg, Selene, and Caly continued the search.

While I was away, they had found and tagged the locations of all but one of the elements we needed: Technetium. Of course, the missing element was also the one we would need to make cryosleep an option. Technically, we didn't need it to complete the journey to Terra, but none of us would live long enough to see our new home world without it. We would have been uploaded to the simulation centuries before arrival and have to wait our turns for resurrection to see the new world.

A tangential thought crept in through my bond with Meg. She was hurting physically, and she was eager to leave this planet. Maybe Hades had overestimated our hardiness—or underestimated the severity of the radiation poisoning.

"Like Selene said, we're almost done here," I reminded Meg, speaking in her mind. I felt like a bit of an ass reassuring her when my case of radiation sickness was far less advanced, but genuine gratitude flowed into me through our bond.

Selene glanced up as I drew near, but her focus quickly returned to the holoscreen hovering above her forearm. "Meg filled you in?"

"She did," I said.

"How's Raiden?" Selene asked, again glancing up, a mere flick of her eyes, quick but long enough for me to spot her genuine concern. I hadn't realized she cared so much.

"He survived the trip," I told her. "He's in the asclypos now. The fungus has invaded his brain, but so far, it's looking treatable."

"Hm . . . good," Selene said distractedly, her brows bunching together as she continued to study the holoscreen.

I scanned the neon-green fungus blanketing everything around us, the floating spores glowing in the dying light like irradiated snow. "Did you know this stuff produces psychic energy?"

"So it *is* Pasitheorales Viride. I thought as much." Again, Selene glanced up at me. "You didn't know about it?"

I shook my head, not volunteering that I kind of *did* know—from first-hand experience. I *shouldn't* have been able to absorb the energy from the fungus that had been growing rampant in the labyrinth. A true Olympian Amazon *wouldn't* have been able to do what I had done.

I made a deal with myself to let Hades and Selene know about the anomaly that was *me* later, when we were far away from this unnerving planet. I would *probably* let them know. Maybe. If it came up.

"I pity Raiden," Selene said. "I've seen people nursed off the fungus's influence. Once it gets a foothold in the body . . ." She shook her head slowly. "It's a long, difficult recovery."

"I gathered as much," I said. But he was safe on the *Elysium* now, already starting down the path to recovery. "How's it going down here?"

"We still haven't found anything to suggest recent occupation of any kind here, Titan or otherwise," Selene said, lifting one shoulder in a halfhearted shrug. "I'm not concerned."

"Glad to hear it," I said as I settled in on Selene's vacant side to peer at the holoscreen.

It displayed a map of the city, with a smattering of tiny blue circles scattered about. Approximately one-fifth of the map remained grayed out, suggesting it had yet to be explored.

"What are we looking at?" I asked.

"Readings from the drones," Selene explained. "We're waiting for them to scan the final portion of the city for Technetium before picking our target."

I studied the map with that information in mind. Empty circles would represent traces of unrefined Technetium, while solid dots would suggest a high likelihood of finding *refined* Technetium, likely already stored in element cartridges. There were no solid blue dots on the holoscreen, which explained Selene's sit-and-wait strategy. Harvesting unrefined Technetium would be far more time consuming than scraping the last dregs of refined Technetium from rusted, spent element cartridges discarded as trash. I crossed my fingers, hoping the drones turned up more promising readings in the unscanned portion of the city.

"Hades set a wellness timer," I told Selene. "We need to be on board the *Argo* and heading back to the *Elysium* in five and a half hours."

A cluster of solid blue dots, faded but filled in, appeared on the edge of the grayed-out section of the map, where the drones were currently scanning. My heart beat faster as excitement surged within me.

"How about that?" Selene said, glancing up at me without raising her face. Her eyes crinkled at the corners, suggesting she was grinning beneath her mask. "We'll be on our way back to the *Elysium* with hours to spare." She raised a hand to the holoscreen, first pinching then spreading her fingers to zoom in on the recently scanned area of the city. "Our fretting prince will be so pleased."

I huffed a laugh, watching as the view on the screen reoriented to display the selected portion of the city. The blue dots multiplied and spread out to make a neat line down the middle of a hexagonal building.

Selene flicked her fingers over the holoscreen, and the view shifted from bird's-eye to street level. The 3D model from the drone scan showed what had once been a tall skyscraper that had, at some point in the distant past, snapped just above the second or third floor, leaving the bulk of the tower lying in the street like the carcass of a felled tree. Broken posts jutted up from the building's stump, their sharp edges softened by what were undoubtedly vines of the fungus and a thick layer of ash.

"It looks like the element cartridges are underground," Selene said, assessing the new data out loud. "But the high concentrations picked up by the drones suggest they're likely not partials."

I straightened, cold washing over me.

"That's excellent news," Caly exclaimed.

Selene raised her head, exchanging a look with me, my mounting dread reflected in her eyes.

"That's not excellent news?" Caly said, her voice threaded with uncertainty.

Selene inhaled deeply, then slowly shook her head.

"No," I said, speaking for Selene. "It's not good news." I looked at Caly. "Technetium is rare and essential for extended long-distance space travel. The element cartridges are high-value items. Full cartridges would never be left behind, especially not in such a volume as this."

Selene turned her face away, staring out toward the part of the city displayed on the map.

"They would, however, be precisely the type of supplies one might stash in an outpost," I added. "Under guard."

Meg approached from behind us, having sensed first my burst of excitement, followed by the mounting dread.

"And," Selene said, "considering the abundant supply of psychic energy generated by the Pasitheorales Viride, I would wager my life that those guards are Titans."

Silence settled over the four of us as we reoriented ourselves to this troubling shift in our situation.

"It's too bad we can't use the energy from the fungus like the Titans can," Meg said, her voice hushed.

I stared at her hard. She knew, obviously. She was in my head just as much as I was in hers. She was digging for information from Selene because I was too scared to do it myself. I feared asking too many questions about the fungus would give me away. If Selene and the others realized I shared the ability to use the fungus energy in common with the Titans, they would undoubtedly start to wonder if I could drain them, too. Could I steal their psychic energy? Could I suck it out of them, just as the Titan had done to their Zari sisters?

Selene suppressed a harsh laugh with a cough. "Tell me about it," she said, shaking her head. "The first time I encountered the stuff—" She glanced at me. "Des and I were part of a team searching the gephyra network for untapped veins of orichalcum." Again, Selene laughed and shook her head, but this time the sound was warmed by her reminiscing.

I couldn't help but smile with her. I missed Despoina fiercely. She was the closest thing I had ever had to a sister, at least before Meg. Despite Despoina being safely stored in the *Elysium's* Vault of Souls, I hadn't visited her in the simulation since that first, unexpected encounter with her consciousness orb in the Omega site. I didn't think I would be ready to face her again until I could assure her that the mess Hades and I had inadvertently made thousands of years ago in our attempt to save our people was cleaned up and that the path to a brighter future was clear.

"I tried for *hours* to access the vast well of psychic energy," Selene said, continuing to recount her story. "Like I would miraculously be different from the others. Like I might be *special*." Her eyes met mine, hers glittering with mirth. "But I couldn't absorb even a hint of it. I couldn't even sense it."

I averted my gaze, scanning the inside of the warehouse rather than give Selene a chance to wonder at the fear in my eyes.

"So, what do you think?" Selene asked.

I could feel the untapped psychic energy thrumming beneath my feet, almost like it was calling to me.

"Cora?"

I forced myself to focus on her face, trying really damn hard to keep my expression blank. To *not* look like I was trying to hide something from her.

Selene glanced down at the map projected above her holoband, then back up at my face. "Should we check it out?"

I weighed the risks, assessing the change in our situation. The parameters of the mission hadn't really shifted. We had gone into this assuming Titans were present somewhere on this planet. Confirmation of their presence in the ruined city—or rather, *under* it—didn't change the fact that they had been there all along, merely that we *knew* they were here. If anything, we were in a better position now, fully aware of the very real danger we faced on this planet.

I nodded, first to myself, then more deliberately for the others to see. I met their eyes, first Meg's, then Caly's, and finally Selene's. "We should call back the drones and scout the area manually," I said. With our hoplon suits muting the energy given off by our bodies, and our orichalcum hoods dampening our mental signatures, we would be harder for the Titans to sense than the drones. "Let's try to find the underground access," I added, thinking aloud. "And see if any Titans come out. It would be nice to get an estimate on their numbers, if possible."

"I agree," Selene said. "Once we have adequate intel, we can reassess. If we need to head back to the *Elysium* for some R&R and to formulate a new plan, we might as well do it with as much information as possible."

I nodded once. "Send the location to the others," I told her. "We'll meet them there."

11

CROUCHED AT THE OUTER edge on the seventh floor of a tower bordering the fallen skyscraper, I peered through the darkness. Veins of fungus surrounded the structures with a dim, unearthly green light, affording me a hazy view of the hollowed-out ground floor of the building sitting atop the underground stash of Technetium cartridges.

Selene had taken up a similar position directly opposite me in a neighboring building. Meg was on the fallen tower, roughly a block away from the target location, and Melyse watched from the sixth floor of another building. The remaining five members of the team were positioned strategically at street level in the surrounding buildings, giving us eyes on every nook and cranny in and around our target.

We couldn't risk venturing any closer—and definitely couldn't actually breach the outer walls of our target building—on the off chance that there was hidden surveillance directly within and around it. Thankfully, the floors of the second and third levels had long since collapsed, leaving piles of fungus-covered rubble on the ground floor, granting those of us stationed higher up a clear view of the interior, illuminated by the eerie green glow from the veins of fungus and the floating spores. Without the ashfall further clouding the air, we had a surprisingly clear view, not unlike what might be seen through night-vision goggles.

If not for the readings from the drones, I never would have suspected that a veritable treasure trove of Technetium cartridges lay stashed beneath these ruins. Pretty much every other part of the city was in better shape than this portion. But then, maybe that was the point. Why would anyone search for a supply stash or underground outpost *here*?

We had gone dark with our tech, shutting down holobands and even our comms patches to prevent any chance of detection, and we were communicating via hand signals and line of sight, none of which would have been possible without the green glow. I estimated we had a few hours left until Hades' wellness timer urged us back to the *Argo*, but there was no way to know for sure without booting up my holoband, and I would need to retreat several blocks into the city to do that. Even without a concrete clock, I could rely on my increasing nausea to mark the passage of time. Meg had already vomited, requiring the removal of her mask for a brief period, but the minimal exposure to the hallucinogenic spores didn't seem to be messing with her head—yet.

Suddenly, excitement surged within Meg. I closed my eyelids and opened myself to the bond so I could see through her eyes.

Where once there had been an unbroken mound of rubble in the one interior corner of our target structure that was blocked from my view, an opening had formed. An entire portion of the debris had vanished, revealing a short, backlit tunnel. The entrance to the underground hideout was blocked by a hologram.

A head appeared, rising from a staircase at the end of the shallow tunnel. As more of the figure appeared, there was no mistaking the glow of neon-green psychic energy marking her form-fitting body armor in an intricate geometric pattern. A Titan. She stood in the mouth of the tunnel, silhouetted by the harsh white light behind her as she surveyed the ruined courtyard.

Another figure emerged from the staircase. Then another, and another, until six Titans stood in two neat lines behind the first, all wearing that distinctive power armor saturated with glowing green psychic energy.

Through Meg's eyes, I watched the Titans march out of the tunnel, the apparent leader remaining behind to reset the holographic barrier concealing the tunnel entrance. They crossed to an exterior doorway on Meg's side of the building.

Up on her perch, Meg ducked behind some rubble to remain out of sight.

Heart hammering in my chest, I pulled out of Meg's mind to survey the situation through my own eyes. From my vantage point, I could see the Titans now, stalking out into the ruined city. They were dispersing. Scattering. Fanning out in all directions. They scanned their surroundings like they were searching for something.

Did they know we were here? Had they somehow detected us? Or had our drones missed some hidden surveillance equipment in the surrounding buildings?

Meg's rising anxiety drew my attention to our bond. Down on the street, a Titan passed precariously close to her position but, thankfully, didn't once glance up to where she was hiding. That suggested they didn't know we were here. At least, not *right here*, watching them.

I quickly reassessed the situation. We could attempt to take out the Titans, but an outright psychic battle would draw out other warriors, if any, that might be hiding underground. If none, once we had cleared the threat, we could breach the holographic barrier and steal the element cartridges. Assuming there weren't more Titans stationed down there, we had the greater numbers. But they had an endless supply of psychic energy. Our only real advantage would be the element of surprise.

There were too many unknowns. Too many disadvantages. If we returned with double the numbers and specialized weapons, we could *maybe* take them out with an ambush. *Maybe.*

I caught Selene's attention with a wave of my arm and, using the hand signal language the Order of Amazons had developed for such situations, relayed my thoughts. *"Seven Titans,"* I signaled. *"Too risky. Retreat."*

Selene shook her head, a sharp cut of her chin to the right, then back to the left. *"Regroup,"* she signaled back to me. *"Sit tight. Wait for their return. Retreat."*

"Shit," I hissed. "Shit. Shit. Shit."

She was right. It would be far too risky to make the trek across the city back to the *Argo* while the Titans were out and about. Meg had the best view of the disguised entrance. If we reconvened at her position, we would know the moment the Titans returned to the underground outpost. Then we could journey back to the ship in relative safety.

"Regroup at Meg's position," I signaled to Selene.

Selene nodded once, then turned her shoulder to me and relayed the order to Melyse.

I slunk backward into the more densely concentrated haze of spores within the building's interior and cautiously made my descent. By the time I reached Meg, the others were already gathered.

Blood smeared down Kyra's chin, suggesting a gushing nosebleed. Even with the respirators blocking the lower halves of their faces, everyone appeared haggard, wilting under the effects of the radiation. If we waited too long for the Titans to return, we could very well wipe out our entire team ourselves, no battle required. We would have to risk venturing through the city while the Titans were out. We wouldn't have a choice.

After another couple of hours passed with no sign of the Titans returning, I caught Selene's eye and coaxed her away from the others with a sideways nod. We crouched together on an exposed post nearby.

"We can't stay here much longer," I said, my voice low, for her ears alone.

Dark purple half-moons colored the area under Selene's eyes, a thick sheen of sweat coated her skin, and small lesions seeped blood across her forehead and cheekbones. I was the only one who had yet to vomit, thanks to my brief reprieve from the planet's toxic atmosphere, but nausea twisting in my gut promised it was coming soon. I didn't need confirmation from my holoband to know we had blown past the deadline Hades had set for us.

I searched Selene's weary stare and hissed, "The radiation sickness will kill us."

"Eventually," Selene said. "But not as quickly as the Titans will if we cross paths with even one of them right now." She rested a heavy hand on my shoulder. "We wait, Cora. We wait, or we die."

I clenched my jaw, wanting to argue.

Selene gave my shoulder a squeeze. "We wait."

12

I CROUCHED ATOP THE husk of the fallen tower, tucked against a steel post, my shoulder and hip pressing into the several-inches thick sheet of cushy, glowing green fungus that blanketed the deteriorating metal beam. The felled skyscraper periodically groaned beneath us as I battled the nauseousness knotting my stomach. It was almost like the deteriorating building was expressing how I felt—awful.

Because I still hadn't vomited or suffered from one of the gushing nosebleeds like the others, it meant I was the only member of the team who remained unexposed to the spores' mess-with-your-head effects. I didn't think I was far behind them, though. My first radiation sore had appeared on my forehead about ten minutes before and continued to weep blood into my eyebrow.

Below, the others huddled together in the cover of the felled tower's interior, curled up on their sides or propped up against some rubble, conserving their energy for the trek back to the *Argo*.

I would have ordered a return to our ship sooner, but the worsening condition of everyone on the team vastly decreased our ability to be stealthy and greatly increased our chance of catching the Titans' atten-tion. And the possibility of fighting them off was laughable. It was more important than ever that we waited until the Titans returned to their underground lair before heading out, even though continuing to wait was less of an option with every passing minute.

I drew my hand across my brow line, wiping away the blood tickling my eyebrow, and switched my focus from the sealed holographic barrier blocking the entrance to the Titans' underground hideout to the streets surrounding this side of the building's exterior.

"Come on, you bastards," I murmured. "Come on . . ."

A spike of adrenaline surged through my bond with Meg, and I tore my attention away from the streets to peer down at her through the tower's carcass. Meg and Selene kneeled on either side of Melyse, who lay stretched out on her back, her body seizing. Selene shoved the Zari Amazon's mask down over her chin and turned the seizing woman's head to the side, allowing the pink foam filling her mouth to flow freely onto the ground.

The seizure lasted a minute, though it seemed like an eternity. When Melyse's violent shaking finally ceased, her body relaxing, Meg looked up at me, her fear oozing into me.

"She's unconscious," Meg said, speaking in my mind. "I doubt she'll wake again." Which meant we would have to carry Melyse back to the *Argo*.

I clenched my jaw, then turned my attention back to the holographic barrier, willing the Titans to return and fighting the urge to order our immediate retreat. We could wait a *little* longer. If even one more of our number fell unconscious, we could still make it back to the ship. Slowly, but we could make it. If we left at that moment, our painfully sluggish return to the ship would make us easy targets for the Titans.

A second weeping lesion opened on my forehead while we waited. A third appeared on my right cheek, just above the top edge of my respirator. At a tickling sensation inside my left nostril, I wiggled my nose. A sudden, gushing nosebleed flooded my mask and poured into my mouth.

I yanked the respirator down and spat blood, spraying crimson on the irradiated fungus. My stomach heaved, and for a few wretched heartbeats, I thought I might kill two birds with one stone and vomit *while* my nose gushed blood. I spat again, and the urge to gag lessened.

I caught movement in my peripheral vision. Just a flicker on one of the side streets leading back to the skyscraper's ruined base.

I hastily secured my respirator over my nose and mouth, gagging at the pervasive coppery scent of blood, and stared hard at the place where I thought I had spotted movement. There was nothing now, just glowing veins of the fungus and eerie shadows among the ruins and rubble.

Had it been a trick of the eye? I hadn't had my mask off for more than thirty seconds, a minute at most. Could the fungus be messing with my head, making me see things that weren't really there?

Again, movement in my peripheral vision caught my attention. Pulse pounding, I snapped my focus to the right. There, in the courtyard, a figure illuminated by the glowing geometric pattern on her body armor stalked toward the sealed holographic barrier.

I fell still, completely and utterly, and watched the Titan.

She pressed her hand against the surface of the holographic barrier. A moment later, it vanished.

I squinted. She had used her psychic abilities to control the hologram. That boded well for us. If she could get in using psychic energy, then so could we—when we returned, after we had recovered.

I glanced down at the rest of my team. Assuming we survived long enough *to* recover.

When my focus returned to the courtyard, I discovered another Titan had joined the first. A third approached from a break in the exterior wall on the opposite side of the structure from us. A fourth, from our side. The first Titan remained at her post by the tunnel entrance, standing watch as each Titan returned and retreated into the tunnel until only one Titan remained unaccounted for.

I squeezed my hands into fists, ceaselessly scanning the courtyard and surrounding streets, searching for any hint of movement. Where *was* she?

A jolt of adrenaline from Meg startled me, and my whole body jerked. I tore my attention away from the Titan posted by the mouth of the tunnel and peered down at Meg, my heart hammering in my chest. I half expected to find her fighting off the missing Titan. But that wasn't what had caused the distress that surged across our bond.

Selene lay slumped on her side, unconscious. I stared down at the grim scene. Now we would have to carry two members of our team back to the *Argo*. And it wasn't like the rest of us were hale and hearty at the moment.

I gulped. This wasn't the worst-case scenario, but it was pretty damn bad.

Meg peered up at me, fear and worry pouring in through our bond. She felt awful—weak and shaky—and wasn't at all confident in our ability to make it back to our ship while hauling two unconscious women.

I held up a hand, one finger raised to tell her to hang on, just for a moment, then turned my attention back to the courtyard of the wasted building. Adrenaline pushed my own physical discomfort aside and sharpened my focus.

The Titan was gone. The hologram was back in place. The tunnel entrance was sealed.

I stood straighter, frantically scanning every inch of the courtyard and the streets and buildings immediately surrounding it. Had the last Titan gone into the tunnel, or was she still out here? What about the one who had been waiting at the entrance? My attention had been elsewhere for ten, maybe fifteen seconds. Barely any time at all. Long enough that all the Titans could have reemerged. Or they could all be underground. There was no way to know for sure.

And it didn't really matter. Either way, we were out of time. We had to move out. Now.

I stared at the hologram sealing the tunnel entrance for a three count, then dropped to a crouch and shakily climbed down to the ground, where the others waited. Meg was able to rouse Selene into semi-consciousness and pulled her up to her feet while I descended, but Melyse was still out cold.

I hurried over to Meg and tucked in close to Selene's side, pulling Selene's arm over my shoulders while Meg supported her on her other side. The others worked together to carry Melyse, though a couple looked like their knees were about to buckle.

"Let's move out," I said, my voice emerging stronger than I felt. "Prioritize speed over stealth," I added, hoping the Titans truly were underground. I scanned the weary faces of my team members, making eye contact with each, then half-dragged Selene out into the street.

Another Zari psychic collapsed during the trek back to the *Argo*. Selene was lucid enough to walk with my support alone, so Meg joined the others to share in the burden of carrying two unconscious women. By the time we reached the ship, everyone was swaying on their feet. *But* we made it without any Titans attacking.

Relief flooded my aching muscles the instant my boot clanged onto the invisible ramp leading up to the cabin of the *Argo*, and by the time I settled Selene in one of the passenger seats lining the side of the ship, I was near tears. Feet dragging, I shuffled to the front of the ship and collapsed into the left-most pilot seat. I booted up the engine while Meg and the others first strapped in their unconscious sisters, then sat and secured their own seat restraints.

I had just finished charting our launch path when Meg settled in the seat beside mine. I noted the rapid rise and fall of her chest and shoulders as she fought to catch her breath. Her hands trembled, and she struggled to latch the final seat restraint. She blinked rapidly, like she couldn't quite focus on the buckle.

"Here, let me," I said, unfastening my own restraints so I could lean closer and help with hers.

Meg's stare met mine as the buckle clicked into place, gratitude flowing through our bond. And then her chest and shoulders convulsed. She tore her mask down, turned away from me, and puked on the floor on the other side of her seat.

I gave her arm a squeeze, then returned to my seat and buckled myself in. "Hang on," I told Meg, glancing at her sidelong. "This will all be over soon."

Meg settled back in her seat and flashed me a weak smile. Her face was gaunt, her skin a wreck of open sores, and her features were slack, her expression dazed.

I returned my attention to the holoscreen displaying our flight path, then laid my hands on the navigation sphere and launched the *Argo* into the sky.

13

M Y HEART RACED AS we broke free of the planet's atmosphere. A moment later, the *Elysium* lit up as active on the comms list pinned in the bottom right corner of the holoscreen. The enormous ark ship winked into existence on the navigation chart, though I still couldn't see it through the viewscreen. I altered our course to aim for the transport airlock at the *Elysium's* stern.

"Hades?" I said, a fingertip pressed against my comms patch to forge a link. "Can you hear me?"

Despite knowing we were heading straight for the ship, the view of nothing but an endless sea of stars ahead had me half convinced the *Elysium* was gone, and my heart stumbled over the next dozen beats. Or maybe that was a side effect of the radiation sickness.

"Hades?" I repeated, an audible tremor in my voice. I tugged down my respirator, fearing he couldn't hear me through the mask. "Are you there?" Tension stiffened every inch of my body as I waited for a response

"I'm here, Cora," Hades said, finally. "The *Argo* just appeared on our charts." He may have said more, but I was having a hard time focusing on listening through the overwhelming rush of relief.

I melted back into my seat, leaning my head against the seatback, my chest shaking with something that was both a laugh and a cry. My hands slipped off the navigation sphere, and the holoscreen split in two.

"Cora? I need you to stay with me," Hades said. "Cora?"

Dazedly, I shook my head, and the ship's controls swayed back and forth, double vision fracturing further. Beside me, four versions of Meg sat slumped in their seats, heads lolling to the side. I squeezed my eyelids shut, then opened them again, attempting to banish the double—quadruple—vision.

"Cora!" Hades' voice was a whip crack.

I blinked, and my fractured vision snapped back to a single, cohesive view, and there was only one Meg sitting beside me. My neck felt rusty, resisting as I faced forward and focused on the navigation chart. The *Argo* had veered off course.

"I'm here," I said, blinking rapidly, then opening my eyes as wide as they would go. I sat up straighter and replaced my hands on the navigation sphere, correcting our course to aim for the rear of the *Elysium* once again. "Sorry."

"I need you to stay with me until you're within the *Elysium's* shields," Hades said, his voice cool, calm, controlled. Had I imagined the panic sharpening his words a moment ago? "Then I can take control of the *Argo* remotely." He fell quiet for a moment, then added, "Stay with me, Cora, just a little while longer."

I coughed, blood spraying across the navigation sphere and the backs of my hands.

"Almost there," Hades murmured. "Almost . . ."

Squinting, I focused on the icon of the larger ship on the navigation screen. It split in two, but I closed one eye to hold off the double vision a little longer. I inhaled and held the air in my lungs.

A behemoth of orichalcum-reinforced steel appeared on the viewscreen, blocking out the stars.

"I've got you," Hades announced victoriously.

I expelled my held breath and let my hands slide off the navigation sphere. I slumped back in my seat, dazedly watching on the viewscreen as the *Elysium* seemed to swallow us whole. My eyelids drifted shut, just for a moment.

When I opened them again, the sound of hydraulics filled the cabin. I twisted as much as I could while still held tight by the seat restraints, craning my neck to peer around my seatback. The rear hatch was opening.

Frowning, I faced forward again, peering through the viewscreen. We were parked in the transport hangar. I couldn't remember passing through the airlock.

With fumbling fingers, I unfastened my seat restraints. I stood, legs trembling so badly that my knees threatened to buckle. I leaned against my seatback and dragged in deep lungfuls of air.

Once I was a little steadier on my feet, I shuffled forward, heading toward the hatch lowering at the back of the ship. As soon as the ramp touched down, I made my stumbling descent.

Hades and my mom waited on the other side of a shimmering energy barrier. I blinked, confused by what I was seeing.

A quarantine field, I realized, like before. Right. That made sense.

At least a dozen Amazons accompanied my mom and Hades, each standing within their own personal quarantine bubbles. The psychics' protective barriers shimmered in a rainbow of colors, reflecting the hue of each woman's psychic energy.

I stopped at the very edge of the silver barrier surrounding the *Argo* and swayed on my feet. "They—" I suppressed a cough, choking on the copper tang of blood. "They need an asclypos," I rasped.

My chest convulsed, and this time, I couldn't suppress the cough. Blood splattered the inside of the energy barrier, not enough mass to break through, sizzling upon contact.

My mom's eyes widened in horror.

Suddenly, I was falling, the transport hanger spinning around me. Hades' face filled my vision, no shimmer of silvery energy obscuring his striking features.

"I've got you," he whispered, his arms secure around me.

My body went limp as darkness swallowed the world.

14

AWARENESS RETURNED GRADUALLY. I groaned and groggily turned my head from side to side. My entire body felt leaden. My arms, legs, and head weighed a thousand pounds each, and my eyelids were so heavy that all I could manage was a flutter of my eyelashes before temporarily admitting defeat. Clean, dry air flowed through my nostrils and filled my lungs, carrying the faintest medicinal scent.

Finally, I managed to peel my eyelids open, and I squinted against the bright light as I took in my surroundings. Metal walls. Seven reclining chairs. Recovery chairs. The motionless forms of slumbering people. One with auburn hair. Selene.

A pulse of adrenaline burned away the bulk of the sedative fog, and I pushed up on my elbows and then curled my body until I was sitting upright in my reclined recovery chair. My mind worked clumsily, fumbling to piece together the fractured memories of leaving Othrys.

I was in a recovery pod in the Med Sector on the *Elysium*. We had made it back, clearly, but how much had the delay cost us?

105

I hastily scanned the faces of the women in the other recovery chairs. Including mine, all eight chairs were occupied, but there had been nine members of the team. Who was missing? Meg lay in the recliner beside mine, our bond as dormant as her unconscious mind. Selene was across from me, also out cold. Caly was beside her, and Kyra was on the other side of Meg. Helyna, Zephyra, and Lyssa—they were here. They had all survived.

But what about Melyse? Hers was the only face I didn't see. She was likely in another recovery pod or still in the asclypos, undergoing another healing session.

Concern for Melyse wasn't enough to temper my relief at having escaped that hellish planet. It was as potent as any sedative, and I relaxed back in my recovery chair and let my eyelids drift shut, savoring how *good* I felt physically. Or maybe it was just the absence of feeling *bad*. No nausea. No burning lungs or shortness of breath. No throbbing, stinging skin.

I inhaled deeply, pleased to find that doing so didn't trigger the urge to gag or cough up blood. Opening my eyes, I turned my head and glanced at the tray table attached to the side of my chair. A water tumbler and a comms patch lay on the polished metal surface.

I reached for the tumbler, placed the straw between my lips, and drank deeply. Cool, refreshing water poured down my parched throat. I paused, breathing hard after taking such a long drink, then polished off the contents.

Once my thirst was quenched, I returned the tumbler to the tray table and picked up the comms patch. I peeled the patch off its backing and stuck it to the skin behind my ear, then pressed a fingertip to the patch to activate it and open a comms channel but hesitated before speaking anyone's name. What if it was the middle of the ship's artificial night and everyone was asleep?

I lowered my hand and again reached for the tumbler, only remembering I had already drained it when I picked it up and felt it was empty. I set it down and dragged my legs over the edge of the recovery chair, letting my feet dangle. Arching my back, I stretched my neck first one way, then the other. With a sigh, I relaxed my spine and scooted closer to the edge until my toes skimmed the cool metal grating on the floor.

I cautiously eased off the chair. My head felt a little light and floaty, but my legs were steady, so I slipped my feet into the slippers that had been set on the floor under the tray table and reached over the table to grab the long, dusky blue sweater hanging on a hook on the wall behind the recovery chair. I shrugged into the sweater, hugging it closed over my thin tunic as I shuffled down the center aisle toward the pod's exit.

With the press of a button, the door panel glided open, and I stepped out into the corridor. Motion-activated lights illuminated the hallway, their muted glow telling me it was indeed nighttime.

For long seconds, I stood in the corridor, unsure where to go. My feet started moving before I had fully decided, but by the time I passed through the wider door from the Med Sector to the ship's broad main corridor, I knew my destination.

I reached the Bridge some ten minutes later but stopped as soon as the double door panels slid open, revealing the dark space beyond. I stood at the very end of the main corridor and peered through the shadows up at the vacant captain's platform. There was nothing for me here.

Turning on my heel, I made my way back down the main corridor, heading for the Residential Sector to check on Raiden. I glanced at the door to Hades' private quarters as I passed, but the yellow frame around the control pad on the wall told me the room was empty. Emi's door was next, but the control pad was set to *do not disturb*. Raiden's was the same, the control pad's subtle red glow taunting me.

Surely it wouldn't hurt to take a tiny peek. To just poke my head in, make sure he was all right, then leave him to rest.

Unable to resist, I reached out and tapped the control pad. The panel flashed a brighter crimson before returning to the subtler, solid rosy glow, and the door panel itself remained sealed shut.

Surprise parted my lips. Raiden's door was locked. Not just from within but sealed with a code.

I frowned, my eyes narrowing, and glanced down the corridor to Emi's door. Why would she have sealed Raiden in? Unless . . . Was his mind still under the influence of the fungus?

I laid my palm on Raiden's door panel, raising my other hand to deactivate my regulator. Closing my eyes, I rested my forehead against the polished metal surface of the door and reached beyond the barrier with my psychic awareness.

I sensed him within. A surface skim told me his mind was quiet. He was asleep. Tempted as I was to delve deeper into his head to discover the reason for the locked door, doing so would likely rouse him from slumber. After all he had been through, he deserved to rest.

Sighing, I pulled my psychic fingers out of Raiden's room and opened my eyes. At least he was alive. I straightened, letting my hand slide down the smooth metal surface, and activated my regulator once more. I stared at the door panel for a long moment, hugging my sweater shut around me, before finally taking a step back.

I glanced up the corridor, toward my sleeping chamber, but the idea of lying on my bed and staring up at the ceiling while my thoughts whirled was utterly unappealing. I had rested enough in the recovery pod.

My stomach groaned with hunger, and I wondered how long it had been since I last ate anything. Frowning to myself, I turned in the opposite direction and headed for the dining room at the far end of the Residential Sector.

The dim glow of the overhead lights spilled into the corridor as I approached the broad, open doorway to the dining room. A pair of Zari women glanced my way as I entered the room. They each lifted their chin in greeting.

I raised my hand in response but moved past them, heading for the middle-aged woman sitting alone in the back corner of the dining room, her brown hair pulled back in a low, loose bun and her eyes glued to a tablet. I wasn't entirely surprised to find my mom there, wide awake while most of the ship slept; she had always been a night owl.

"Hi, Mom," I said as I approached her table.

My mom looked up, her eyebrows raising. A heartbeat later, her lips spread into a broad grin. She set down her tablet, pushed her chair backward, and stood, rushing forward to throw her arms around me.

"I was so scared," she said, squeezing me tight. "You were gone for so long, and we didn't know what was going on down there."

"I know," I said as I returned the hug, tucking my chin over her shoulder and breathing in her familiar scent. "I'm sorry. Do you know if—" I hesitated in asking about Melyse, just for a moment, fearing the answer. "Is Melyse all right? She wasn't in my recovery pod."

"She's fine," my mom said as her arms loosened. "The fungus got into her head, so Hades wanted her isolated for the time being." My mom pulled back enough that she could see my face, and her eyes searched mine. "When you were down on the planet, when you blew past the deadline on his timer, Hades was—" She shook her head. "I've never seen him like that. He's always quiet, but this was different—scary quiet."

I knew exactly what she meant.

A crease formed between my mom's brows. "What happened down there? We checked your holobands, but you must have powered them down." Again, she shook her head. "There's no record at all of your activity for the last seven hours of the mission."

My stomach rumbled, loud enough to interrupt her. "Sorry," I muttered.

The corners of my mom's mouth turned down. "There are some blue-ish-berry biscuit-scone things over there," she said, pointing toward the long counter that ran the length of one side wall of the dining room. I followed her line of sight to the small, clear box filled with golden cubes of bread sitting beside the beverage dispenser. "I'm calling them *biscones*," she said, looking inordinately pleased with herself about the name. "They're actually quite good."

"Yum," I said, flashing her a tight smile before hurrying over to retrieve a handful of the biscones and fill a tumbler with water. When I returned with my midnight snack, my mom had reclaimed her seat at the small corner table. I pulled out the chair adjacent to hers and sat as well.

"So?" she asked, her eyebrows raised.

I tore off a piece of one of the too-square-too-be-natural pastries and popped it into my mouth. Soft, buttery, and faintly sweet, with a rich flavor that definitely didn't taste like blueberry. I frowned as I chewed. "Is that *raisin*?"

My mom's stare told me she hadn't been asking about what I thought of her latest culinary creation and that she knew *I* knew it. Her expression softened anyway, and she shrugged. "It's been hard to program the right flavors with the depleted element cartridges."

"I know," I sighed. "At least we found most of what we need before . . ."

My mom tilted her head to the side, her brows bunching together. "Before *what*?" she asked, leaning forward slightly. "Sweetheart, what happened down there?"

I swallowed my bite and sat back in my chair as I sipped some water, settling in to give her a recap of the events that had led to my team's extended trip down on Othrys. She was quiet after I finished. I picked apart the last remaining biscone, arranging the crumbs into a miniature model of the ruined building housing the concealed tunnel.

"So, Hades was worried?" I asked, looking up from the crumbs.

My mom barked a laugh and crossed her arms over her chest. "You could say that," she said, shaking her head. Her stare hardened on me. "How are you feeling now? You weren't as sick as the others." She leaned forward, resting her crossed forearms on the table. "Melyse almost didn't make it."

I nodded to myself. She had passed out first, so it made sense. My focus drifted past my mom to the wall behind her. Where was Hades, anyway?

"Do you have any lingering nausea?" my mom asked, dragging my attention back to her.

I shook my head. "I feel fine," I added with a one-shoulder shrug.

The Zari women shared a laugh, and we both glanced their way. My mom was still watching them when my focus returned to her. "I went to check on Raiden, but his door was locked," I said, asking about him without actually asking anything.

My mom's attention snapped back to me, concern evident on her face.

"Have you seen him at all?" I asked.

My mom shook her head. "I've barely seen Em either," she said. "Only in passing. She's still in a personal quarantine bubble, so she has to keep her distance, and she's always in a rush or too preoccupied to say more than a few words."

"Huh," I said. If Emi was still quarantining herself, then Raiden's mind *must* have still been under the influence of the fungus.

My mom shrugged her shoulders and grunted softly. "I get it," she said. "She almost lost him—her only child—and he's still struggling to break free from the influence of that fungus, *which* Hades assures me is perfectly normal in such an extreme case. Honestly, Cora, if it was me in her place and you in Raiden's, I would be acting exactly the same way."

I stared down at my crumb model, battling the urge to apologize for something that hadn't even happened.

My mom drew in a deep breath, exhaling through her nose. "Hades brought Em the holodisk containing the recreation of the crash site a few hours ago," she volunteered. "I haven't seen him since, but you could check in with him—see if *they* spoke more about Raiden's recovery."

I nodded absently. "Yeah, I will." After a moment, I pushed back my chair and stood. "Thanks, Mom."

She offered me a closed-mouth smile that did nothing to drive away the concern shining in her eyes. "Don't wander around for too long, sweetheart," she said. "You need to rest after that ordeal."

I laughed bitterly as I scooted the now empty chair closer to the table, then wiped the crumbs into my waiting hand. "I've *been* resting for the last—" I frowned, cocking my head to the side. "I don't actually know how long."

My mom glanced at her watch. "About twenty-six hours and two sessions in the asclypos," she said, then raised her eyebrows. "The others required three sessions."

Gripping the top of the chair back, I slowly shook my head. Luck had been on our side today. Or yesterday, I supposed. If the Titans hadn't returned when they did, leaving the way back to the *Argo* clear for us . . . well, I didn't want to think about that.

"What did you do with Tila?" I asked, imagining my burly dog trapped in my quarters for nearly two days.

"She stayed with me," my mom said in a no-nonsense tone, like it was the most obvious thing in the world. "She's in my room now, sleeping," she added, her raised eyebrows telling me I should head back to my room and do the same thing.

"I'll take it easy," I said, raising my hands partway in surrender. "Promise." I flashed her a small smile. "I just can't sleep anymore right now."

"All right," my mom said begrudgingly.

I started to turn away.

"And please, *please* seriously consider searching for the Technetium we need somewhere else," my mom added.

I paused, one hand still resting on the top of the seatback. "I will," I said, nodding once. "Promise." I flashed my mom a small smile, then crossed the dining room to drop my handful of crumbs in the waste chute to be broken down to their component elements for reuse before heading for the exit.

I wandered into the Genetec Sector in search of Hades, then back to the Med Sector, but didn't find him in any of the usual places. I did come across Fiona, perched on a stool in the laboratory, holding both the caged Tsakali scout and the remains of the pirate Titan. Fiona sat slumped forward over a worktable, using her crossed arms as a pillow, deeply asleep.

The scout huddled in its cage in the back corner, the dimmed lights glinting off its ever-watchful eyes. I would never understand how she had managed to relax enough to fall asleep with *that thing* watching her. But, considering Fiona's tendency to work herself into a state of exhaustion, I doubted relaxing had anything to do with her current slumber. She had likely crashed. Hard.

Shaking my head, I smiled to myself and left the lab. I paused in the corridor outside the lab and deactivated my regulator to do a quick psychic sweep of the ship, searching for Hades. I tilted my head back when I sensed him almost directly above me. The only place up there of note was the observation deck, two levels up.

Steps faster than before, I wound through the Med Sector to the lift near the main corridor and rode it up two levels. The lift door slid open with a whispered *whoosh*, and suddenly there he was. Hades stood near the reinforced glass with his back to the lift, dressed in his usual gray tunic and pants, his hands clasped behind his back. His silver-blond hair hung loose, the damp locks leaving darker patches on his shoulders, suggesting he had recently showered.

Physically, he was still, almost completely motionless save for the gentle rise and fall of his shoulders with each slow breath. But inside, he was a tsunami. His emotions crashed into me, wave after wave of fear and anxiety, grief and anguish.

Rooted in place on the lift, I hastily activated my regulator. I considered leaving. Riding back down and retreating to my quarters. I told myself that Hades likely wanted to be alone, anyway. That was probably why he had come up here.

Except . . .

I couldn't bring myself to reach for the control panel to shut the lift door. I squeezed my eyelids shut, and a tear snuck between my lashes to glide down my cheek. With a shaking hand, I wiped it away, then stared down at my damp fingers. At the remnant of *his* pain.

Pulled forward by some unknown force, I stepped out of the lift and quietly crossed the deck, my slippers *shushing* against the metal grating.

Hades peered over his shoulder as I approached. His eyes were red-rimmed, his features weary. Even so, the corners of his mouth tensed and rose when he registered who had intruded on his solitude. He scanned me from head to toe, his gaze assessing. When his focus returned to my face, there was no hiding from the emotion shimmering in those ice-blue depths, even with my psychic gifts muted.

Wordlessly, I stopped at Hades' side.

He glanced down at my regulator, his stare lingering on the soft amber glow signaling that my psychic gifts were dormant. "You don't have to hide from me," he said, his voice a low murmur.

His gaze locked with mine, and my breath caught in my throat. Tentatively, I raised my hand to my regulator and touched the tip of my index finger to the stone.

Unlike with everyone else, I never felt like I was invading Hades' privacy when I skimmed his surface thoughts. He never worried about what I might glean from his mind. There were no emotional walls. No mental barriers. Not anymore. Not since a lifetime ago, when the worst of the secrets between us had finally come out. He wasn't afraid of me seeing his deepest, darkest thoughts. Quite the opposite, in fact. He welcomed the prospect. He wanted me to know him—*all* of him. Even the scary parts.

My chin trembled as I traced my fingertip around the regulator stone, unleashing my powers.

Hades' emotions slammed into me, and I held his stare as tears welled in my eyes and broke free. Not from the fear or the grief I had sensed mere moments ago. Those were all but muted, driven away by relief. By admiration. By *love*.

I swallowed roughly, then licked my lips. My arm trembled as I reached behind Hades and pulled one of his hands free. "Thank you," I whispered as I threaded my fingers between his.

Hades bowed his head. A moment later, he returned to staring out at the stars.

I did the same, letting his thoughts and emotions flow through me.

Hades appreciated Raiden for his sacrifice but knew that were he in the same position, he wouldn't have made the same decision. He would have demanded we go together, not deceive me and martyr himself. He had learned his lesson there. I followed that train of thought as he recalled the moment, thousands of years ago, when he had been on the verge of doing just that, but I had seen his dangerous thoughts and begged him—ordered him—to *not* sacrifice himself.

My throat tightened, and my heart hurt.

Hades worried about Raiden and how saturated his body had been with the fungus. It was the most extreme case he had ever seen, a fact he had been holding back from everyone. He feared how devastated I would be if, after everything, we were to lose Raiden.

He considered other locations to search for the Technetium we still needed.

He wondered what exactly had happened to me and my team down on *Othrys*.

And beneath it all, he loved me, quietly and unconditionally.

Warmth spread throughout my chest, and a fresh string of tears spilled over the brim of my eyelids. But these tears were mine, and mine alone.

Despite his whirring mind, Hades didn't feel the need to voice any of those thoughts. He wasn't willing to let anything disturb this stolen moment. *Our* moment.

Neither was I.

So we stood together, hands joined, and silently stared out at the stars.

15

"WE SHOULD REST," HADES said eventually, breaking the spell cast by the starlight.

The faintest hint of crimson burned along the edge of the observation window. Soon, Acheron would impinge on our view of the stars.

"The ship will begin to wake in a few hours," Hades added. He looked at me, his gaze burning paths over the side of my face. "Can I walk you to your room?" The innocent question masked a not-so-innocent opportunity.

Yes, I wanted to scream. And I didn't want him to leave me at my door. I wanted him to come into my quarters, to fill the cramped space with his oversized presence. His quiet weight. His solemn intensity. I was desperate to lose myself in this distraction. And Hades was more than willing.

Except, I refused to *use* Hades. I wouldn't let our relationship be tainted by *anything*, especially not by my tangled feelings about Raiden. By all the worry and anger and hurt knotted in my belly. And if I went with Hades now, it would be.

I glanced down at our joined hands, then raised my eyes to meet his. "I'm going to stay here for a bit longer," I said, my voice hushed. "You go." I offered him a smile, a faint curving of my lips. "I need to clear my mind."

Hades bowed his head, and I sensed his understanding. He turned toward me, sidestepping to stand in front of me, close enough that I had to tilt my head back to maintain eye contact. "I'm here," he murmured, pressing our joined hands against his chest, directly over his heart. "And I see you." His stare flicked down to my regulator and its glowing electric-blue stone, and I sensed the strangest mix of yearning and regret from him.

My breath hitched as I understood what he desired. Intimacy, yes, but not merely the physical kind. He wished there was a way for him to know me, inside and out, as I knew him, even as he was glad that such a thing was impossible. He feared what he might sense in my mind, what he might learn about my feelings toward him.

He was completely unaware that such a thing actually *was* possible. A closely held secret of the Order of Amazons. A deep, dark taboo. If a psychic and a non-psychic both touched a regulator while it was deactivated, it would form a conduit between the two, allowing the non-psychic to sense the psychic's thoughts and emotions as well.

I had never attempted it, and the prospect of doing so with Hades both terrified and thrilled me. I was unsure whether I truly wanted to experience such a deep connection with Hades or whether his desire was influencing my own, but my heart was suddenly racing. I couldn't do it now, not when my emotions were tangled in knots over the Raiden situation. I would never do that to Hades—let him into my mind and heart, only to see how preoccupied I was with another.

Searching Hades' gaze, I inched closer and rose on my tiptoes until my mouth hovered a hairsbreadth from his. "And I see you," I whispered, sliding my hands over his shoulders to overlap behind his neck. And then I leaned in, pressing my lips against his in the sweetest, gentlest of kisses.

Hades closed his eyes and rested his forehead against mine, tension vibrating through his body. His desire for more warred with his ironclad restraint. He refused to press me for fear that doing so would push me away.

I let my heels drop, and Hades opened his eyes. He lifted our joined hands to his mouth to press a kiss to the back of mine, then lowered and released my hand. "Goodnight, Cora."

My cheeks flushed at the heat in his stare. At the desire in his blood. At the promise in his heart.

Hades stepped around me, and I turned partway, watching him cross the observation deck. Even after he was gone, I continued to stare at the lift's polished metal door, fighting the urge to go after him.

I was afraid. A coward now as much as I had been all those millennia ago. Hades already had one foot in the door to my heart. If I let him all the way in and then lost him—a prospect that felt all too real after the disaster with Raiden—I feared the grief would destroy me.

Finally, I turned back to the observation window to gaze out at the stars. My heart ached in Hades' absence, when only a moment ago he had filled me so completely with his whole self. I raised a hand to activate my regulator, preferring to feel nothing at all.

16

A HALF HOUR AFTER Hades left me on the observation deck, I made my own way down to the Residential Sector. I passed the door to Hades' quarters without glancing at the control pad, then passed the door to Emi's quarters.

And stopped mid-step. Even in only my peripheral vision, it was impossible to miss that her *do not disturb* had been turned off.

I backed up a step and deactivated my regulator to run a quick psychic scan of the space beyond. But Emi's sleeping quarters were empty.

I glanced up the corridor. The frame around the control pad to the door to Raiden's room still glowed red. I could always channel psychic energy into the door controls and override the lock, but Emi must have sealed Raiden in for a reason. Maybe because he was still under the influence of the fungus. Or maybe because his immune system was compromised. Or maybe the reason was one of a million other things I couldn't think of because I had zero medical expertise.

Releasing a resigned sigh, I continued down the corridor. I skimmed my fingertips over the smooth surface of Raiden's door as I passed.

He would always be Emi's number one priority. She would never have anything but his best interests at heart, and there was nobody I would trust more with his recovery.

I let my hand fall away from the wall and continued down the corridor. I retreated into my sleeping quarters, where I quickly washed up, then fell into the narrow bed. I curled up on my side and closed my eyes, hoping for deep, dreamless sleep.

I WOKE SCREAMING AND sat bolt upright in bed. My heart hammered in my chest, and my throat felt raw. I touched my fingertips to my cheeks, and they came away wet with tears.

I had fallen asleep in my quarters only to "wake" in a dream that I was back in the transport hanger as Raiden boarded the pirate shuttle. Except, this time, he was grinning. Laughing. Gloating. Like he had won. Like he had beaten me.

"Ugh," I groaned, flopping onto my back on the mattress. I jerkily kicked the blankets off my legs so they bunched at the foot of the bed and stared up at the ceiling, replaying the dream—the nightmare—in my mind.

Irrational rage heated my blood. Raiden hadn't done that. He hadn't been the least bit happy about flying the decoy ship away. In my mind, I knew the truth, but the warped dream had fooled my heart.

With a frustrated growl, I sat up, then stood and stomped into the bathroom, hoping a frigid shower would cool my temper. It did not.

But it did clear my head enough that I could wade through the anger to the root source. I had been feeling flickers of outrage since Raiden left, but I only now understood why.

Raiden had betrayed me. At least, that's what it felt like.

He had ambushed me and stolen my choice to fight at his side. The odds of survival aboard the decoy ship may have been shitty, but they would have been a thousand times better with us working together than they had been for Raiden flying off on his own. He gave up—on life. On us. On me.

I quickly dried off and dressed, opting for my hoplon suit over the more comfortable and casual loose-fitting tunic and pants. I needed the physical armor to reinforce my emotional walls.

Determined to see Raiden, I emerged from my quarters. The bars of light running along either side of the ceiling glowed with bright, artificial daylight. I peered up the corridor, my focus locking on the red-framed control pad beside Raiden's door.

I deactivated my regulator as I stalked up the corridor and stopped in front of the door panel, extending my psychic awareness into the space beyond. Once again, I only sensed Raiden within, but his mind was dormant, like he was sleeping. Still.

The residual anger from the dream dissipated until all that remained was worry.

Brow furrowing, I activated my regulator, muting my psychic gifts, then touched my comms patch. "Emi," I said, forming a private link with her. "I'm outside Raiden's room, and I need to see him. Can you come down here and unlock the door?"

"I'll be right there," Emi said through the comms patch, her words rushed. "Wait for me, Cora. I'm on my way now."

I moved across the corridor and leaned back against the wall opposite Raiden's door, crossing my arms over my chest. A few minutes later, Emi rounded the corner at the end of the corridor, once again contained within the shimmering silver barrier of a personal quarantine bubble. I pushed off the wall, letting my arms drop to my sides. Strands of hair strayed from her usually neat braid, and dark circles stained her under eyes.

"Em," I said, studying her weary face as she approached. "Is he—" I was afraid to ask, fearing the worst—that he wasn't recovering well. Or at all. "How is he?"

Emi's eyes met mine, then affixed on the control pad, like she was confirming it was still locked. "His recovery is taking longer than I had hoped, but he's getting there," she said, her steps slowing. She stopped with her back to the door panel, facing me. "I know you want to see him, Cora, but now really isn't a good time. He's undergoing a treatment—"

My eyebrows rose. "In *there*?" My focus shifted past her to the door panel, like I could see through it to the man concealed within. "You put a mobile asclypos *in his room*?"

"I—" Emi licked her lips. "Yes," she said, nodding. "It was easier than sealing him in a quarantine bubble to take trips back and forth to and from the Med Sector."

I took a small step closer to her. "What's wrong with him, Em? Is it just the fungus, or is it something more?"

"It's the fungus," she said, hugging her middle. "It warps his perceptions of, well, everything." She sighed, her shoulders slumping. "He just needs some more time. So, if you don't mind . . ." She turned away from me, blocking my view of the control pad with her body.

Emi's hand moved over the grid, and a moment later, the door panel slid open.

"Em, wait," I said, rushing forward.

Emi slipped into the room and flashed me an apologetic smile as she pressed the button to shut the door from within. I caught a glimpse of Raiden lying on his back on his bed before the panel slid shut right in front of my face.

I gaped at the door, stunned that Emi had effectively just slammed it in my face. Pressing my lips together, I reached for the controls to open the door, but a red frame flashed on around the control pad. She had locked me out.

I narrowed my eyes and glared at the glowing red frame. My hand had risen to my regulator, seemingly of its own accord, and the tip of my index finger hovered over the amber regulator stone. I fought the urge to unleash my psychic gifts and slip into Emi's mind to at least see Raiden through her eyes. But she would sense such an invasive mental intrusion, and she would not forgive me easily.

Gritting my teeth, I forced my hand to lower. Emi would never do anything to hurt Raiden. If she said he needed more time, then he needed more time.

Even knowing that, I couldn't make myself leave. So, I settled in to wait, once again leaning back against the opposite wall and crossing my arms over my chest. I stared at the red-framed control pad like I could see through it and into the sealed room.

About thirty minutes later, the crimson frame winked off.

Acting on impulse, I deactivated my regulator and hastily channeled psychic energy into my hoplon suit to enter stealth mode and become invisible to the naked eye.

The door panel glided open, and Emi emerged.

I snuck forward, slipping past her and through the open doorway into Raiden's room, edging around the shimmering quarantine barrier shielding the bed half of the room. A moment later, the door panel slid shut. I sidestepped into the corner of the small room and turned to watch as a red frame flared to life around the door's interior control pad. Wide eyed, I stared at the door controls, a little stunned at what I had just done.

But then I sensed him behind me. Raiden. Awake.

Moving slowly, silently, I turned around.

Raiden sat on the edge of his narrow bed, his back straight and his hands resting on his knees. His expression was blank, and just like on the *Argo*, his mind felt off somehow. Still him, but his surface thoughts felt hollow. That had to be the influence of the fungus.

I couldn't help but wonder if more was going on with him. He had already been suffering from PTSD from his time in the military. Had whatever happened to him after he flew the decoy ship away from us traumatized him enough that he had retreated deeper into his mind? If that were the case, there was a chance I could help. Or even better, I could ask Meg to take a peek. She was up and out of the recovery pod, working out in the training room, and I sensed her willingness to help through our bond.

"Let me try first," I told her, speaking in her mind. And then, unable to resist, I stopped channeling psychic energy into my suit, allowing myself to be visible once more.

Raiden blinked and focused on me, his placid expression unchanging, though I caught a whiff of mild resentment coming from him. I frowned, taken aback by the unexpected emotion.

"Hey," I said lamely, forcing a gentle smile. His stare remained locked on me as I stepped forward. I hesitated, pausing before passing through the quarantine barrier to quickly create a thin field of psychic energy to shield me from any stray fungus spores, then continued across the cramped room to ease down on the bed beside him. "How are you?" I drew one leg onto the mattress and angled my body to face him. "I mean, are you all right?" I searched his face. His eyes. "Are you in pain?"

Raiden shook his head, though I wasn't sure which question he was answering. Was he saying he wasn't in pain or that he wasn't all right?

"I, um, would like to understand what happened to you." I raised one hand, touching two fingertips to my temple. "Can I—" I looked pointedly at his own temple. "Take a look inside?"

He didn't say no. But when I reached for him, he flinched.

My hand froze, my fingers splayed as if in surrender. "Okay," I said, lowering my hand. "I'll stay out of your head."

Hostility radiated off Raiden, flaring hot but fading quickly.

My chin trembled, and I fought back tears. That hostility had clearly been aimed at me. Was it born of the fungus's influence, or had it come from Raiden himself? It was impossible to tell the difference. Emi was right—I shouldn't have come in here.

I blinked rapidly as I stared at the opposite wall and tried really damn hard not to take his reaction personally. "I don't know what happened to you after you left," I said. "But I saw your ship down on the planet. You must have suffered unimaginable things, and I am so, *so* sorry for that."

Raiden said nothing. He just continued to stare at me. I watched him out of the corner of my eye.

"I wish . . ." I inhaled shakily. "I wish I had been with you," I said. "I *should* have been with you." I dragged my stare back to him. "Why did you do it? Why did you leave me here? Together, we might have been able to—" I shrugged, then let my shoulders slump. "I don't know."

"It wouldn't have made a difference," he said, his voice cold, unfeeling. "You couldn't have saved me. Not on your own."

I jutted my jaw forward, my anger rising. I shoved it down, away. "You don't know that," I said calmly.

"The others who were on the planet with you," he said, his focus drifting away, dismissing me. "Are they back now?"

I let out a silent guffaw. Was he implying that I couldn't protect him here, either? That I wasn't *enough*?

"Yeah," I said, my voice tight. "We're all here."

"Good," he said without looking at me. "I'm tired. You should go."

My spine straightened, my heart stuttered, and I expelled a bitter, breathy laugh. "Yeah, sure," I said, standing.

I reminded myself that Raiden had been through something truly horrific. It wasn't *him* dismissing me. It was the fungus, or maybe his trauma, or some combination of the two. There were good reasons not to take his dismissive indifference personally. Logically, I knew that. But my heart didn't.

Stiffly, I crossed to the door and reached for the control pad, preparing to psychically override the lock. I paused, my hand hovering over the controls, and bowed my head. "I'm sorry, Raiden," I said softly. "I'm sorry I dragged you into all this—you and your mom and everyone else." I felt like I was choking on my heart. "I just—I'm sorry." I closed my eyes, freeing a string of tears.

And then I sent threads of psychic energy into the control pad. A moment later, the lock disengaged. When I opened my eyes again, the red frame around the control pad was gone. I punched the button to open the door and slipped out of the room, pausing only to close it from the outside before releasing the bubble of psychic energy I had been maintaining and fleeing up the corridor.

My heart hammered in time with my hurried steps. I couldn't get away from Raiden and his resentment fast enough. My fast walk turned into a stumbling jog, which increased to an all-out run.

I had no idea where I was going, just that I needed to be away from there. Away from Raiden and the way I had felt around him. Like I had failed him. Like I was worthless.

Like I wasn't enough.

17

M EG WAS WAITING FOR me on the center mat by the time I stormed into the training room, Selene and Helyna flanking her, practice dorus in hand. Meg had sensed my need to unleash my pent-up rage, and she and the others were ready.

I deactivated my regulator and, rather than reaching over my shoulder to draw the doru sheathed on my back, thrust my right arm out to the side and reached out with tendrils of psychic energy. A practice doru flew across the room from the stand near the wall and smacked against my palm. I closed my fingers around the smooth metal staff and reactivated my regulator, never missing a stride.

The women sparring on the outer mats stopped what they were doing and turned to watch. Some moved closer, but not by much.

I spun the doru as I stalked onto the center mat toward the trio of waiting warriors. They broke apart, bending their knees and shifting their own practice dorus, preparing for my attack. With a guttural cry, I launched myself at my opponents.

I spun in the air, altering the trajectory of my initial attack from Meg to Helyna, who stumbled backward as I swung my doru around for a narrow miss. Meg came for me from behind, and I twirled and squatted, intending to sweep her legs out from under her. She leapt over the staff easily. I struck at her with my elbow, my knee, my doru, but she was too quick, able to read my intentions through our bond. She had the advantage, as I had to fend off peripheral attacks from Selene and Helyna, as well, and couldn't focus entirely on what I sensed in Meg's mind.

At the last second, I chucked my doru at Meg, changing from a side kick aimed at her to a back handspring that landed with my thighs wrapped around Selene's neck. I twisted my upper body, hauling her down to the mat, and squeezed my leg-lock around her throat tighter, clamping off the flow of blood to her brain.

Selene tapped the outside of my thigh twice with her open hand, signaling that she was out of the fight. I relaxed my legs, releasing her from the chokehold. Breaths heaving and heart pounding, I climbed to my feet and turned around while Selene rolled onto her side, coughing.

Meg stood at the center of the mat, a doru in each hand. Her eyes narrowed, and I could feel her through our bond, assessing my need to continue the fight.

"Stay out of my head," I ground out.

The corner of her mouth tensed. "I couldn't if I tried," she snapped, and then she tossed one of the practice dorus at me.

I caught the staff easily and settled into a defensive stance as Meg planted the end of her doru on the mat and sprang forward, feet aimed for my chest. I barely managed to duck and roll away. She was a tornado of attacks after that, and it was all I could do to block her strikes. There was no opening for offensive moves. I was too tangled up in my own mind to pay attention to what was going on in hers or read her moves before she struck.

It wasn't long before I miscalculated Meg's intent, and she caught me in the gut with the end of her doru. The air whooshed out of my lungs, and I dropped my staff and bent double, sinking down to one knee.

"Had enough?" Meg asked, her boots coming into my field of vision on the mat.

A hollow laugh shook my chest. I reached for my discarded practice doru, my fingers curling around the smooth metal, and I raised my head to peer up at Meg. "Not even close."

Meg's lips spread into a vicious grin. Her entire body tensed a moment before she struck again, whipping her doru around like she was trying to take off my head.

I rolled to the side, easily regaining my feet. We circled one another, chests and shoulders rising and falling with our heavy breaths.

Meg attacked. Again and again and again. With each round, more Zari Amazons gathered around the center mat to watch. And ever so slowly, the hurt and anger that had driven me to this fight faded into the background until there was only physical sensation, the movement, the fight.

"Had enough?" Meg asked again, the butt of her doru pressed against my throat while I lay sprawled flat on my back on the mat, my own doru well out of reach. I had lost track of how many times she had uttered those two words.

The muscles in my arms and legs burned from overuse, and my body ached from the dozens of strikes she had landed, even through the protection of my hoplon suit. "Yeah," I rasped, nodding as much as I could with the staff digging into my windpipe.

Meg pulled her practice doru away and thrust out her hand, an offer of help rather than of pain. My palm smacked against hers, and with a grunt from both of us, she hauled me up to my feet. Once I was standing, she released my hand to grip my shoulder. Her expression softened, filling with the empathy I could feel flowing through our bond.

I covered her hand with mine, sending her a silent thanks for literally beating me back to my senses.

Meg's focus shifted past me toward the entrance to the training room.

I glanced over my shoulder. My mom approached the center mat, Tila bounding ahead of her. The gathered Zari women parted to let them both through. Tila circled me, barely managing to stop herself from jumping on me as she wiggled her butt and reared back repeatedly. My mom stopped on the edge of the mat and scanned me with the assessing stare of a mother, her expression concerned.

Two sharp claps cut through the silence, followed by a deep bark from Tila. "Show's over, Amazons!" Selene said, her voice raised. "Get back to work!"

The women surrounding the center mat dispersed, and I turned to face my mom. "Did they tell you to come?" I asked, scratching Tila's head. The pit bull had planted her butt on the toes of my boots and was leaning her muscular body against the front of my legs.

My mom nodded. "Selene thought you might need me." My mom glanced down at Tila, the corners of her mouth twitching. "Or, rather, *us*."

Chin trembling and eyes stinging, I swallowed the rising swell of emotion. I clenched my hands into tight fists and set my jaw. I *really* didn't want to fall apart in the middle of the training room, surrounded by the warriors I was supposed to be leading. At least, not more than I already had.

My mom rushed forward and wrapped an arm around my shoulders.

Sensing it was time to go, Tila sprang to her feet and trotted toward the doorway.

"Come on, sweetheart," my mom murmured, drawing me toward the exit. "Let's get out of here."

We moved up the corridor and ducked into the next room over, the overhead lights flaring to life. The smaller space was filled with extra mats and training gear.

My mom pressed the button on the control pad to shut the door panel, then guided me toward a rolled-up training mat. We sat; her arm still curved protectively around my shoulders. Tila stretched out on the floor at our feet, her heavy head resting on my boots.

I stared at the pile of damaged practice dorus discarded in one corner of the room, recalling Raiden's face, that apathetic expression, his simmering resentment, and the cold, dismissive words he had spoken. The ache in my heart was dulled by the beating I had taken at Meg's hands, but it was still there.

My next inhale was far shakier than the last. I blinked, sending tears streaming down either cheek. My shoulders slumped, and I collapsed against my mom, curling into her. She wrapped her other arm around me, pulling me in closer.

"Did you see him?" she asked, her voice hushed.

"Uh-huh," I said through a choked sob. I focused on taking slow, deep breaths until some of the tension left my chest and I could speak. "He was cold," I said, my voice high and tight. "And kind of cruel." It felt absurd to say the words out loud, like I was crying to my mom about a boy being mean to me when literal civilizations were at risk.

But this wasn't just any boy. This was Raiden, who I *loved*.

"I know he's all messed up in his head from the fungus, but I think he resents me for what happened," I finally admitted. "For what he had to do." A single, despondent laugh shook my chest. "Maybe he *should* resent me for that."

My mom stiffened. "Even if that's the case—which I highly doubt—tell me one thing, Cora," she said, her voice low and even. "Did you have a choice?"

I sniffled, pulling back enough that I could see her face. "What do you mean?"

Her gaze was steady on mine. "Could you have stopped him?"

My eyebrows bunched together.

"You were half dead and out of psychic energy," she said. "What could you have done, really? Could you have fought him off when he put you in a headlock? Could you have forced your way onto the shuttle?"

"I don't—" I shook my head, thinking through what I might have done differently to change the outcome of the situation.

I could have never invited Raiden to accompany me down to the transport hangar. I could have flown the decoy ship away myself without having told him about the faulty autopilot. I could have begged him to take me with him.

Again, I shook my head. "I don't know," I whispered.

Fingers gentle, my mom brushed a sweaty lock of hair away from my forehead. "He made his choice," she said. "You are not responsible for his actions, nor for the consequences of the choices he makes. He chose to fly that ship away *without you*. He knew the risks, and he chose the option that was most likely to result in your survival."

"But it wasn't his choice to make," I wailed.

"But he *did* make it," she said. "He made the choice, and it's done, and now we have to pick up the pieces and fit them back together as best we can."

I rested my head on her shoulder. "What if they don't fit together anymore? What if *we* don't fit together anymore?"

My mom exhaled a sigh and squeezed my shoulders. "That's the risk we take in opening our hearts to others. Loving another is the greatest risk of all."

I squeezed my eyelids shut, refusing to accept the truth in her words.

"Give him time, Cora," my mom said. "Be gentle with him. And in that time, please, please, *please* be gentle with yourself, as well."

18

"Now that we know they're there," Selene said from my right, "it shouldn't be difficult to lure them out and ambush them. With some well-placed UV grenades to kill the veins of fungus and cut off the Titan's supply of psychic energy and some EM grenades to dampen their powers, we can extend our advantage by a minute or two. Plenty of time to take them out."

Shaking my head, I gripped the curved edge of the navigation console and arched my back. My body ached from the brutal session in the training room earlier that morning. I stared up at the holographic model of the local galaxy and where we might find the Technetium we still desperately needed.

My focus shifted past the model to Hades, the only other person on the Bridge for this impromptu strategy meeting. He stood on the far side of the navigation console, his thoughtful expression as he listened to Selene the only thing keeping me from arguing against returning to Othrys.

Yes, we knew we could find what we needed down there. But the stash of Technetium cartridges was guarded by a full unit of Titans with access to an endless supply of psychic energy. The idea of attempting to loot their supplies seemed absurd to me. Even with all the EM and UV explosives in the armory, I couldn't imagine willingly returning to Othrys to ambush the Titans, especially not now that we were aware of their virtually bottomless supply of psychic energy.

But Hades was listening, and he had always been extremely rational and realistic when considering options and weighing odds. The fact that he was even considering this plan made me think that the chances of finding enough Technetium elsewhere before we ran out were worse than I had previously realized.

Hades finally noticed my attention was on him, and his stare locked with mine through the semi-transparent 3D model.

"Cora?" Caly said, pinging me through my comms patch.

My stare lingered on Hades a moment longer. I touched my comms patch and turned my back to the navigation console. "Yeah?"

"Have you seen Kyra or Helyna?" Caly asked. "They were supposed to meet me in the training room, but I've been waiting for fifteen minutes, and they're not here. Their comms patches aren't registering in the system either."

I frowned, my eyes narrowing. That would mean they had taken their comms patches off for some reason, likely to sleep or to shower. "Did you check their rooms?" I asked. "Maybe they're still feeling worn down."

"I'm on my way to the Res Sector now," she said. "It's just so unlike them to do something like this, especially without notifying me. They're usually so responsible."

I nodded to myself. "If they're not in their rooms, gather a few others and run a psychic sweep of the ship," I said, giving her permission to run the psychically invasive search. "There's only so many places they can be. We'll find them."

"Will do," Caly said. "Thanks."

I crossed my arms over my chest and faced the navigation console once more.

Selene and Hades watched me, eyebrows raised.

"Sorry," I murmured, pressing my lips into a closed-mouth smile.

"Anyway," Selene continued, "the trick would be to make sure we draw all of them out at once. We need to eliminate them all before any of them have a chance to tap into the psychic energy from the fungus. Any stragglers—any Titans hanging back, outside of the dead zone created by our grenades—could pose a serious threat to the mission."

Leaning my hip against the edge of the navigation console, I frowned, looking from Selene to Hades and back. "So, we would have to take them all out with one coordinated strike before they realized they were under attack," I said, my voice flat. "*All of them.* That's not going to be easy, especially when we can't draw on our own psychic powers until the last second." Again, I shook my head. "I really think—"

"Cora?" Fiona said through my comms patch. "Do you have a sec?"

My stare remained locked with Selene's, and the rest of my argument lodged in my throat. Irritated, I jerked my hand up and touched my comms patch. "Make it quick, Fio," I said. "This isn't a good time."

"Oh, sorry," Fiona said in a rush. "It's just that I can't find Stasya. She's usually here waiting in the lab, but . . ."

My hackles rose, and my focus drifted past Selene. "And she's not on the comms network?"

"Duh," Fiona confirmed. "I checked the life scan of the ship, too. She's not in her room."

"Huh." I pinched my lower lip. That made three people who had gone MIA. I couldn't help but think of the pirate incursion, and a surge of dread made me think this was more than a coincidence. "Find an Amazon and ask her to do a psychic scan of the ship," I said, trying to keep the mounting alarm from my voice. I would have done it myself, except I needed to get back to the strategy meeting with Hades and Selene. "Tell her I gave the order."

"Aye aye, captain," Fiona said before disconnecting.

"What's wrong?" Hades asked, drawing my attention his way.

"I'm not sure," I said, my eyebrows bunching together. "A few people aren't where they're supposed to be."

Hades' eyes widened, and Selene's narrowed as she inhaled to speak.

"Cora?" Emi said through my comms patch, her voice frantic.

My heart beat faster, spooked by Emi's tone. I held up a finger, signaling for Selene to hold that thought, and touched my comms patch *again*.

"I've got a bad feeling about this," Selene muttered.

Hades pressed his lips together, his stony expression speaking volumes.

"I'm here, Em," I said through my comms patch. "What is it?"

"Have you seen Raiden?" Emi asked.

"I—" The admission that I had snuck into his quarters caught in my throat. I licked my lips, then swallowed roughly. "Yes," I admitted. "I snuck into his room earlier, but I was only in there for a few minutes. He didn't want me there." When Emi didn't immediately respond, I added. "I'm really sorry, Em. I just—"

"Did you lock the door when you left?" she asked, cutting off my babbled apology.

Chills cascaded down my spine, and I stood ramrod straight. I thought back to my flight from the Residential Sector. I recalled pressing the button to shut the door panel, but I definitely had *not* reset the lock.

"He's not in his room?" I asked.

"He is not," Emi confirmed. I didn't even ask about his comms patch. She wouldn't have contacted me if she had been able to locate him through the ship's comms system.

Four people were unaccounted for. First the three Zari psychics, and now Raiden.

"Cora," Emi said, her tone turning my heart leaden. "We have to find him *immediately*. You saw him. He's not—" She hesitated. "He's confused, and he can't be allowed to roam freely."

"I understand, Em," I said, my voice sounding hollow to my own ears. "We'll find him."

I disconnected with Emi and took a moment to gather my flailing thoughts. The last time people had gone missing on this ship, we had been under silent attack from a cloaked Titan. Was this another incursion?

I couldn't help but think back to the Titans on Othrys. To the moment I had looked away from the tunnel mouth, and they had vanished into their underground hideout and resealed the holographic entrance. Or so I had assumed.

But what if they *hadn't* gone underground? What if they had reemerged during that moment of distraction? What if they had cloaked themselves, followed us back to the *Argo*, and hitched a ride to the *Elysium*? Had they already taken out Kyra, Helyna, and Stasya? Had they snuck into the Residential Sector, targeting Raiden? Was this the trap we had been initially expecting, snapping shut around us?

Or had Raiden caught wind of the attack and gone out looking for them? Right-minded Raiden would have known he couldn't take on even a single Titan on his own, but he was so twisted up in his head that I feared he would try to do just that.

I swallowed, nearly choking on my rising dread, and turned to face the navigation console.

Hades and Selene watched me, wearing twin expressions of alarm.

"Four of our people are missing, including Raiden," I said. "We may have been infiltrated by the Titans." I deactivated my regulator with a sweep of my fingertip.

Selene did the same, and as soon as she had access to her gifts, I felt her sifting through the surface levels of my mind, bringing herself up to speed on the details of the situation in a matter of seconds.

I touched my comms patch again, pinging my mom. "Where are you?" I asked once we were connected.

Peripherally, I watched Selene hurry around the navigation console to fill in Hades on the necessary details she had gathered from my mind.

"I'm in the dining room," my mom said, sounding slightly distracted. "I dropped Tila off in your room for a nap, then headed here. Lunch isn't going to program itself, and I've got a dozen hungry Amazons waiting patiently for their food."

I nodded absently. "Okay, good," I said. "We may have a situation, but you should be safe enough there." Especially with a dozen psychics on standby. "I'm on my way," I added. "Whatever you do, Mom, don't leave the dining room. And if you have a psychic hood, put it on."

She was quiet for a moment, the silence between us ringing. "Are there Titans on the ship?" she asked, no longer distracted.

"Maybe," I said. "We're not sure, but something weird is going on, so just stay put." As an afterthought, I added, "And tell the others with you to pull their hoods up as well."

"Already done," she said. I figured they must have seen my mom equip her hood and followed suit.

"Good," I said. "See you soon."

I disconnected and turned my attention to Selene and Hades. From Selene's mind, I skimmed that she was planning on heading to Fiona in the lab. Through my bond with Meg, I sensed that she and Caly were prepping the Amazons to sweep the ship for Titans. But what to do with Hades? We needed to make sure that all of our most vulnerable people were safe.

An image of Hades unconscious on the floor of the Bridge during the pirate incursion flashed through my mind's eye. I refused to let something like that happen to him again.

With strings of psychic energy, I summoned his protective hood from the arm of the captain's chair up on its platform. I caught the hood easily and tossed it across the navigation console to Hades, distorting the projected hologram. Hades caught the hood and quickly secured it around his neck before pulling the orichalcum-laced fabric up to cover his silver-blond hair.

I drew my own protective hood over my head and nodded to Selene. Hers was already up.

Selene turned and jogged away.

I looked at Hades. "*You're* with me," I told him. "Let's go."

19

I RACED DOWN THE wide main corridor of the *Elysium*, Hades trailing behind me. Our steps slowed as we approached the door to the Residential Sector, and we waited for the motion detector to sense us. As soon as we came to a complete stop, the door panel slid open.

Hades and I hurried into the narrower passage of the Residential Sector, barreling around the corner to the corridor that led to the dining room. I skidded to a stop and thrust my arm out to the side to block Hades from hurtling past me.

Raiden stood in the corridor ahead, just outside the doorway to the dining room, his back plastered to the wall. He took a deep breath, then another, before twisting his upper body and lobbing something about the size of a baseball into the dining room. A brilliant flash of white light flared from within the dining room.

I turned away and raised a hand to shield my eyes. Beside me, Hades did the same. A heartbeat later, my psychic gifts stuttered, fluttering like the wings of a stunned bird after crashing into a window.

Hades reached out to grip my arm tightly. "That was an electromagnetic grenade," he hissed.

I stared at him, my eyelids opened wide and unblinking. "The Titans must be in there," I said, waiting for my psychic senses to flicker back to full power.

Any Titans within the dining room wouldn't be so lucky. Their gifts would be deadened for another thirty seconds or so. Raiden would need help taking out the Titans before their powers returned.

"Raiden, wait!" I called ahead as I spun away from Hades and started up the corridor again, pulling my arm free from Hades' grasp. I made it three steps before stopping dead in my tracks.

Raiden glanced at me for a fraction of a second, the heat of battle burning in his eyes, then tossed another grenade into the dining room before once again ducking behind the corridor wall. He clapped his hands over his ears, but I was too stunned to react.

That *had not* been an EM grenade. That was a plasma grenade. Panic surged within me.

My mom was in there.

Hades caught my arm and tugged me to the wall, blanketing my body with his own as a deafening blast exploded in the dining room. The concussive wave slammed into us. I clung to Hades, my eyelids squeezed shut and my ears ringing.

My breaths heaving, I peeked past Hades' shoulder, blinking as I focused on the scene further up the corridor. Smoke billowed from the doorway. I could just make out Raiden's silhouette as he plunged into the dining room.

Why would he do that? Even if a Titan was in the dining room, our people were in there too. *My mom* was in there.

Something was very wrong with this situation—with Raiden. Fear gripped my heart in a tight fist.

I turned my face toward Hades, who rested his forehead against the wall, opening and closing his mouth like he was trying to get his ears to pop. "Hey, Hades," I hissed, gripping his shoulder tightly. "Are you all right?"

"I will be," he said, finally focusing on me.

"Okay, good." I gave his shoulder a quick squeeze, then released it. "Stay here, and stay down," I said in a rush as I slid out from between his body and the wall.

The *zap* of a laser pistol firing was followed closely by a chorus of screams, and I glanced over my shoulder toward the dining room as I skipped backward.

"Stay here!" I repeated, then turned and ran up the corridor, drawing my doru from the sheath on my back in one smooth motion.

More shots fired, and I leaned forward, all-out sprinting, even as I channeled psychic energy into my doru to charge the focus crystal at the top of the weapon. With a thought, I extended the staff to its full length a moment before hurtling through the doorway and entering a scene of pure chaos.

My steps slowed, then stopped completely as I surveyed the destruction within the dining room. Bodies lay strewn all over the place, some whole but more in pieces. Blood and gore spattered the walls amid the char marks marking the space like a black starburst, and mangled tables and chairs littered the periphery of the room. Raiden was nowhere in sight.

Breathing hard, I scanned every body and body *part*, searching for Titans and their distinctive body armor, but all I saw were Amazons in hoplon suits. The enemy must have evaded Raiden's attack.

Unless . . .

I shook my head, physically refusing to believe Raiden had done this to our own people.

"Please..." The voice was weak and shaky, but no less recognizable to my ears. My mom. She was in the prep space, tucked behind the main dining room.

I hurried across the larger room, picking my way over the slippery, blood-soaked floor. I jumped at the sound of a laser pistol firing in the back room and nearly lost my footing. When I reached the doorway, I stumbled into the prep space, mostly dominated by a food generator taking up the entire back wall, and stopped dead. It took my brain a few eternal seconds to process what I was seeing.

My mom lay on the floor in front of the food generator, unmoving.

Raiden stood over her, a laser pistol in hand, the nozzle of the gun aimed at my mom's head.

Ever so slowly, I shook my head, my focus shifting from Raiden and his laser pistol to my mom. To her terrifying stillness. To the blackened hole seared through her forehead. To the blood forming a macabre halo on the metal floor beneath her.

My brain stalled, unable to comprehend the scene.

I opened my mouth. Shut it. Opened it again. I looked at Raiden and continued to shake my head.

None of this made any sense.

Raiden's coldhearted stare shifted from my mom to me, and the laser pistol followed a heartbeat later, his arm whipping in my direction. He took aim for a headshot.

I flinched at the next *zap* of a laser pistol but didn't feel any pain.

A blazing white beam of light shot through Raiden's forehead. His grip on his weapon slackened, and the gun dropped to the floor a moment before his knees gave out. He collapsed on the floor, sprawling out beside my mom, a matching hole in his forehead.

I gaped, staring at the pair lying on the floor. Instinct forced me to turn, to look behind me, seeking the wielder of the weapon that had taken Raiden down.

Emi stood in the doorway to the dining room, one arm extended before her, a laser pistol gripped in her shaking hand. She looked like an angel in her pristine pale gray tunic and pants, untouched by the bloody massacre in the room beyond. Her long, tidy braid trailed over her shoulder, her black hair standing out in stark contrast against the light fabric, and tears streamed down her cheeks. She stared at Raiden, at her son, at his body lying on the floor.

Emi's arm drooped, and she slowly lowered the weapon. Her focus shifted to her best friend's body—my mom's body—lying beside Raiden's.

"I thought I could fix him," she said, her voice flat, distant.

I didn't think she was talking to me. I wasn't sure she even knew I was there.

Until finally, she focused on me. The agony in her stare gutted me. "I'm so sorry," she whispered. And then she bent her elbow and raised the laser pistol, aiming it at her own temple.

"No!" I shrieked, lunging for her.

But I was too late to stop her from pulling the trigger. All I could do was catch her as she fell and hold her as the light faded from her eyes.

20

I STARED DOWN AT Emi's slack face, too stunned to act. Too stunned *to think*. Dazedly, I raised my head and looked at Raiden. Looked past him to my mom. I stared at her face. At her relaxed expression. Her parted lips. Her open, unseeing eyes. The hole seared through her skull, through her brain.

I blinked, unable to comprehend what had just happened.

"Cora?"

I sucked in a ragged breath and dragged my attention away from my mom's face to glance over my shoulder. Hades stood in the doorway to the massacre beyond, his focus locked on me.

"There were no Titans," someone said. *I* said, except it felt like someone else was speaking.

"Yes," Hades said cautiously. "I can see that." Not once did his focus drift away from me, so how could he see? How could he see *them*?

I returned to looking at my mom, into her glazed-over eyes. Her dead eyes. Raiden's dead eyes. Emi's dead eyes. They all stared back, accusing me. Blaming me. Like only now, in death, did they realize their mistake in loving me. Only now could they see me for what I truly was. A curse. A harbinger of destruction. The thing that would kill them all.

My love killed.

The truth was unavoidable when the evidence lay limp and bloodied all around me. Everyone I loved was dead.

Everyone. Emi. Raiden. My mom. Dead.

Save for one man. One survivor.

Gently, carefully, I shifted Emi's body from my lap and eased her down onto the floor. My entire body trembled as I stood, a two-handed grip on my doru, and faced the person I had loved the longest.

Hades stepped into the room, raising his hands slowly, like he was approaching a skittish animal.

"No!" I wailed. I shook my head and sidestepped, moving away from him. Around him.

I couldn't let him get any closer to me. I was a disease. My touch was death. And him—I couldn't lose him, too. I couldn't bear to see his glazed stare. His vacant eyes, like Emi's and Raiden's and my mom's.

I wouldn't survive losing him. Not after this. After everything.

"I can't," I rasped as I backed toward the doorway, my heart banging against the inside of my ribcage. My teeth chattered. I couldn't stop shaking.

"Cora, please," Hades implored, again stepping toward me. Fear crashed into me. His fear.

Had he finally realized the truth? Did he understand what I was? What loving me would do to him? He had every right to be afraid.

Something inside me bent, groaned, then finally snapped. I backpedaled through the doorway to the dining room. My heel caught on something, and I stumbled backward. My right boot slid out from under me on the slick floor, and I dropped to one knee, the doru clanging on the floor as I planted my hands in a pile of warm, squishy guts. The stink of bowels coated the inside of my nostrils, and I suppressed a gag.

"Cora," Hades said, my name a plea.

I looked up at him, and suddenly I couldn't breathe. First my mom, then Raiden, and then Emi. Hades would be next.

He would be next.

He *would be* next.

If I didn't get away from Hades now—right now—I would lose him, too. In an hour. Tomorrow. In a year, or in a thousand. I. Would. Lose. Him.

Gasping for air, I scrambled to my feet and spun away, using my doru for support as I skidded over the slippery floor toward the exit. I stumbled through the doorway, sliding across the clean metal floor, and crashed into the opposite wall.

"Cora!" Hades shouted, the agony in his voice gutting me.

I used the wall for support as I fled, refusing to look back. I had to get away. From here. From them. From *him*.

When the soles of my boots no longer slid over the metal floor, I pushed off the wall and ran away from that place of death as fast as my feet would carry me. With each stride, I retreated further into myself until the grief and horrific memories grew distant. Until they belonged to someone else. Until I was outside of myself, looking in, watching the distraught woman racing through the warren of corridors.

I was a player, and this body was an avatar.

This was a game. Not real. Didn't matter.

The agony no longer suffocated me.

I could finally—*finally*—breathe.

My pace smoothed out, my legs steadier with each lungful of air. Free of the suffocating despair, I was able to think through what had happened and what I would do next. How I would protect what was left of the people I loved. How I would protect what was left of *my mom*. She was dead but not gone. Not yet.

I needed weapons. Lots of weapons.

With a focused thought, like pushing a button on a controller, I retracted my doru and reached over my shoulder to slide the shortened rod into the sheath on my back. I slowed as I closed in on the main corridor, waiting for the automatic door panel to glide open.

Once it opened, I hurried across the broad main corridor and stopped in front of another polished door to a lift. I jabbed the button on the control pad to call the lift, then waited. Waited. Waited.

I studied my reflection in the polished metal door. My avatar. The black of her hoplon suit was shiny with blood, and crimson smears marred the ghostly pale skin of her face. Her eyelids were opened as wide as they would go, and her blue irises looked electric and wild.

"It's going to be all right," I told her and offered her a tight smile.

She smiled back, but it didn't touch her haunted stare.

The door panel slid open, and she vanished. I stepped onto the lift without another thought about her and rode it down to the lower levels. I stopped in the armory on my way to the transport hangar, overriding the lock with a jolt of psychic energy.

I marched inside and grabbed an ammunition bag out of the bin just inside the doorway, then dove into the deadly stacks. I moved between the rows of floor-to-ceiling storage units, scanning the labels on the cabinets and drawers and searching for what I needed.

Robotically, I pulled a drawer open, revealing a tray of silver, base-ball-sized orbs tucked into individual padded compartments. Electro-magnetic grenades. I plucked a dozen of the EM grenades out of the drawer and tucked them into the bag, then moved on to the UV grenades and then on to the plasma grenades until the bag was so heavy that the strap dug uncomfortably into my trapezius.

I hitched the strap higher onto my shoulder, then stalked back up the armory's central aisle toward the door. I paused to nab a holster and a pair of laser pistols off the secured racks on the wall, then left the armory, making my way down the corridor toward the transport hangar.

The *Elysium* was my mom's last hope. Without this ship—and the simulation stimulating the people stored in all those consciousness orbs in the Vault of Souls—she would die. Not just her body but her very essence. The woman who had raised me would fade into nothing. She would cease to be.

And Hades . . .

The barriers compartmentalizing my emotions wavered, threatening the much-needed distance I had forged between my awareness and my body. For a heartbeat, I was there, truly present, no longer operating remotely. I missed a step and stumbled into the corridor wall.

Hades would go down with this ship.

I couldn't let that happen.

It was within my power to ensure the *Elysium* had everything it needed to complete the journey to Terra. It might cost me my life, but that was a price I was willing to pay to ensure this ship and its precious cargo survived.

I slammed reinforced barriers down, sealing my emotions away. The comforting sense of remoteness, of separation, slid back into place, and I straightened, stepping away from the wall.

I strode into the transport hangar, crossing all the way to the inner airlock door, passing the *Argo* parked nearby. I opened the airlock bulkhead using the manual control pad set in the wall. As soon as the door panel started to glide open, I turned and ran back toward the *Argo*.

I boarded the ship, punching the button to raise the ramp without missing a step, then stashed my heavy ammunition bag in a floor compartment near the pilot's seat. While the engine fired up, I secured the laser pistol holster around my waist, then sat and placed my hands on the navigation sphere, skipping the usual preflight checks.

I lifted the ship off the hangar floor and guided it into the airlock, where I set it down once more. I slipped out through a side hatch and hurried to the control pad to seal the airlock just as Meg barreled into the transport hangar. But she was too late. I raced to the exterior door controls to set it to open on a fifteen-second delay. The light bars lining the frame surrounding the exterior airlock door flashed red, and an alarm blared in time with the flashing warning that decompression was imminent.

I ran back to the *Argo* and climbed onto the ship, yanking the hatch shut and sealing it with barely two seconds to spare. The lights lining the frame around the exterior airlock flared solid red, and the door split down the middle to open.

I settled in the pilot's seat, strapped myself in, adjusted my protective hood over my head, and placed my hands on the navigation sphere. I pressed my palms into the sphere, launching the *Argo* into space as I fled from the *Elysium* and the last remains of my ruined heart.

21

I FLEW THE *ARGO* down to Othrys with single-minded determination, no pesky fears or worries or grief bogging me down. The mission was clear, my resolve absolute. Without the Technetium to refill the depleted element cartridges, the *Elysium* wouldn't make it to Terra. There was a ready supply right here. We had a problem, and the solution was obvious.

I was a player, guiding my avatar through her quest. The difficulty level for this game was set to *impossible*, but I had beaten plenty of games at that setting before. This would be no different. The lack of a respawn element would make the mission more difficult, but the challenge would only make the accomplishment sweeter in the end.

I flew the cloaked ship through the ruins of a city that remained nameless to me, checking my progress on the navigation chart every few seconds as I closed in on the location of the Titans' underground lair. Since there was only one of me to cart the supplies back to the ship, I planned to park as close as possible to the final target. It was dusk, Acheron having already set beyond the barren mountains lining the horizon, but the red glow from the dying star still illuminated half of the sky.

Slowly, carefully, I guided the *Argo* into the hollowed-out bottom floor of a skyscraper a block away from the base of the fallen tower. The exterior wall on one side of this building had sloughed off entirely, leaving the interior exposed and open to my ship.

I set the *Argo* down on the fungus-covered rubble within the shelter of the skyscraper, then powered the ship down until only the cloak and dampening shield remained. Moving quickly and methodically, I secured a respirator over my mouth and nose before unfastening my safety restraints.

Once I was free, I slipped off my seat to crouch near the floor compartment holding my stash of weapons. I pulled the ammunition bag out of the recess, stood, and hoisted the strap over my shoulder. It was a lot to carry. *Probably* overkill. But in one-shot missions like this, where there was no chance for a respawn and failure meant immediate game over, *overkill* became exactly what was needed.

Shoulder straining under the weight of the loaded ammunition bag, I made my way to the back of the ship and punched the button to lower the ramp. I descended the ramp, careful to keep my steps soft, and remotely closed the ship once I was on solid ground. I watched until the ramp was up and the ship was sealed, then slowly backed away. Between my fifth and sixth steps, I passed beyond the reach of the ship's cloak, and the *Argo* winked out of sight.

I backed up a few more steps, scanning the area to make sure there were no obvious signs of a cloaked ship being parked there. I double-checked, then scanned the area again, but found nothing. Satisfied, I turned and snuck out of the building, delving back into the abandoned city.

I trekked toward the crash site in the crater on the far side of the city, a couple of miles away, sticking to the buildings for cover and only moving out into the open when necessary. I had considered setting up my trap in the crater but figured it would be the obvious play. Besides, there weren't many hiding spots beyond the wrecked ship, and I certainly wasn't planning on ducking out *within* the blast radius. I wanted to cut off the Titan's ability to access their gifts, not *my own*.

On the navigation chart, I had spotted a large, circular building a few blocks away from the crater. It appeared to be some sort of stadium or amphitheater, similar in layout and state of ruin to the Colosseum in Rome, and it promised ample hiding places, both for me and for the pieces of my trap.

The ancient, decaying buildings groaned as I passed through them. Another, quieter buzzing noise persisted in the back of my head, but it was easy enough to ignore.

It was full dark by the time I rounded the corner of a tower leaning precariously to one side and the target structure came into view. It was like a skeletal alien recreation of the Colosseum built of reinforced steel and covered in neon-green veins of irradiated fungus.

I surveyed the amphitheater as I made my way up the street between two towering buildings. More of the round structure became visible with each step, and I wondered what it had looked like before this place had been abandoned by the Tsakali. Before the facade had crumbled away and Pasitheorales Viride had taken over everything.

I passed through one of dozens of open archways built in the exterior wall of the amphitheater and ducked into the outer portion of the building. Florescent spores clouded the air, and curtains of the fungus blanketed the posts and beams, hanging down in strings and sheets where I assumed there had once been walls, turning the interior into a hazy, diaphanous labyrinth.

I shouldered my way through a curtain of fungus, moving deeper into the amphitheater. I passed through three more barriers, and I pushed the last glowing curtain aside with one arm to reveal the sprawling, open space at the center of the structure. I took several more steps into the open arena, then turned in a slow circle, surveying everything.

This had definitely been a place for large groups to gather and watch *something*, though what, exactly, I couldn't say. Even without the endless rows of ascending seats that had undoubtedly once fanned out around the open arena, it was easy enough to imagine thousands of people packed in all around me. To hear the roar of a long-ago crowd.

The ground within the vast, open area was lumpy with miscellaneous rubble and covered in a thick carpet of ash cut through by glowing vines, just like every other inch of this forsaken city. A small smile touched my lips. This location was perfect for what I was planning.

I moved farther into the heart of the amphitheater, stopping when I was halfway to the midpoint. I shifted the ammunition bag to my front and opened it partway. The fastening was the same type as was used for a hoplon suit, like a seamless high-tech zipper, and as my finger moved over the top of the bag, releasing the seal, a flash of memory rammed into the wall protecting my mind. The barrier shivered.

Raiden stood before me, stare heated as he watched me drag my fingertip down the front of my hoplon suit.

My heart clenched, and I was suddenly short of breath. I pressed an open hand to my abdomen and bent double, squeezing my eyelids shut. I shook my head as though doing so might dispel the unwanted memory and the emotions that tagged along with it.

Gradually, my mental walls steadied, blocking out everything that could distract me from my mission. I straightened and drew in lungfuls of filtered air, reinforcing my mental walls, pushing them back further, creating more separation between my emotional self and my unfeeling avatar.

After another breath, I reached into the bag, felt around until I found the right shaped object, and pulled out an EM grenade. I set it on the floor of the arena, tucked into a bed of ash in a cranny in the rubble. I moved around the arena, placing nine more EM grenades on the arena floor in the form of a circle.

Once those were all in place, I crossed to the very center of the arena, reaching into the bag as I walked. I pulled out one more grenade—UV, this time—and set it down. I created a larger circle out of the plasma grenades, surrounding the circle made up of EM grenades, then paused to survey my work. None of the grenades were visible, at least not from my current vantage point.

I walked all the way around the open space, double-checking the layout of my trap, trotting forward to adjust the positions of a few of the explosives. Finally, I was satisfied, and I retreated to the warren of tunnels surrounding the arena to finish the job.

I made a slow circuit around the amphitheater, sneaking through the fungus-lined corridors as I tucked the remaining UV grenades into hidden nooks and crannies. Once I was done, I stood in one of the arched openings connecting the arena to the outer labyrinthine corridors, placed my hands on my hips, and triple-checked my work.

When detonated, the UV grenades would obliterate the fungus in the immediate area, while the EM grenades would temporarily suppress the Titans' ability to access their psychic powers. Once the Titans were vulnerable, the plasma grenades *might* deal a death blow if any Titans stood close enough to one when it detonated. But it was far from a sure thing, especially with their body armor. To be safe, I was planning on having to finish them off myself after they had been stunned and hopefully injured by the blasts from the plasma grenades.

I rubbed my hands together. The bones of the trap were set. I marched back into the center of the arena to move the final pieces into place.

Turning in a slow circle, I channeled psychic energy, forming thin threads that connected the strategically placed grenades in such a way that detonating any one of them would lead to a chain reaction that would detonate all the others. Once they were all linked by psychic fuses, I held my hands together in front of me, palms up, and willed psychic energy to pool in my cupped hands. Electric-blue energy crackled and writhed above my palms in the shape of an orb, swelling until it was as large as a basketball.

Slowly, carefully, I crouched and set the ball of energy on the floor in the center of the arena, and then I stepped back. I couldn't feel the mass of psychic energy with my hood up, but such a compact, concentrated ball of the stuff would act as a beacon to any who could sense it.

And on the off chance that the surge of psychic power hadn't been enough to get the Titans' attention, I reached into the neck of my hoplon suit and pulled my regulator out by its chain, then unclasped the orichalcum case shielding its distinctive energy signature. They wouldn't be able to resist the lure of the chaos signature radiating from the regulator stone.

After ten heartbeats, I swept my fingertip around the stone in my regulator to activate it, deadening my psychic gifts, then snapped the case shut around the pendant and tucked it back into the collar of my hoplon suit. When the Titans arrived, I didn't want anything distracting them from that tasty feast of the electric-blue orb of psychic energy.

Unhurried, I crossed the arena and squatted in a sheltered nook of rubble in the outer corridors of the amphitheater. I had baited the trap. All that was left to do was to wait.

22

EYELIDS SQUEEZED SHUT, I huddled in my hiding spot, as still and quiet as possible, and listened. Each inhale and exhale was carefully controlled. Each shift of my head to alter the angle of my ears was achingly slow.

I was relying on my ears to let me know when the Titans had arrived. I couldn't lower my hood to unleash my psychic radar. While it would allow me to sense the Titans coming, it would also alert them to *my* exact location. *I* wasn't the bait. *That* was the electric-blue ball of psychic energy sizzling in the center of the arena.

As I sat and waited, I replayed the events that had driven me down here. With the clear head of an outsider, I could recognize what must have happened on the *Elysium*. The Tsakali must have captured Raiden and somehow brainwashed him, possibly even completely wiped his mind and implanted a new, foreign consciousness akin to what we had done with Henry Magnusson. It wasn't actually Raiden who killed my mom, but a Tsakali assassin wearing his body as a disguise in order to breach our shields and walk among us on our ship.

Except, Emi had seen through the ruse. There was no fooling a mother's heart.

I supposed it was a blessing that they had all sustained injuries to the head. Their consciousnesses would likely be too corrupted by the damage to their brains for clean extraction, which meant the versions of Emi, Raiden, and my mom that would be uploaded to the simulation and eventually reborn on Terra would have no memory of the most recent atrocities.

A faint scuffing sound drew my attention to the right, and my eyelids snapped open. Someone was here, within the outer corridors of the amphitheater.

I stretched out my neck to peek over the heap of ash and rubble concealing me. Through the gaps between the glowing green vines of fungus that hung down in place of the decayed walls, I caught sight of a tall, shadowed silhouette one corridor over, heading in my direction.

I filled my lungs, then held my breath.

The figure stopped, leaving a sliver of its armor visible through a break in the irradiated vines. It didn't look like the body armor the Titans had been wearing earlier. It was bulkier, and there were no glowing green geometric designs.

I squinted and leaned forward. *This* appeared to be Olympian armor. Specifically, it appeared to be the matte black power armor usually worn by the men filling the ranks of the Order of Gargareans, my people's force of elite non-psychic warriors. Except, in place of the usual helmet, a dark hood covered the interloper's head, concealing any further identifying characteristics. Was that one of the orichalcum-laced pirate hoods? I couldn't tell if I was seeing things or if the fabric of the hood really did shimmer with a faint hint of gold as the apparent Gargarean turned their head.

The figure started moving again, away from me now.

I released my held breath in a controlled exhale and slowly rose to my feet to creep after the intruder. Whoever they were, they didn't belong here. Not right now. Not when I was on the verge of blowing this amphitheater to smithereens.

Silently, I drew the laser pistol from the holster on my left hip. I moved on quiet feet down the corridor parallel to the one used by my unwanted guest, sneaking ever closer. The intruder's height and what was visible of their general build suggested they were male. He was louder than me, and I concealed the noises of my movements by synching my steps with his.

The armored intruder stopped again, and I hung back as he peered around like he was searching for something.

As soon as he turned his head away from my hiding spot, I leapt out from behind a post wrapped in glowing green veins of the fungus and shoved the interloper backward against another post on the far side of his corridor. I pressed my left forearm crosswise against his throat, cutting off his air supply, and jabbed the nozzle of my drawn laser pistol into his gut. This close, not even the thick armor would protect him from the blast.

Eyes narrowed to a hard glare, I peered up at the face concealed under the hood. I looked past the respirator and stared into familiar ice-blue irises.

Hades. He was here.

I stumbled backward, shaking my head.

Hairline fractures formed in the walls in my mind, threatening the mental and emotional distance keeping me sane and focused.

I took another step back and squeezed my eyelids shut, like I could erase what I had just seen. Like I could convince my mind to stop playing tricks on me. Like I could rewrite reality and make it so he *wasn't* here.

But when I lifted my lids again, Hades' stare still bored into me. *He* still stood before me, and the confirmation of his presence rattled the walls in my mind.

"Hades?" I hissed.

The cracks in my protective mental barriers deepened, thickening as they spread. Again, I shook my head. My eyes opened wide, and the walls within me started to crumble, unleashing the flood of grief and despair I had damned up deep within myself.

I squeezed my eyelids shut as what had been a buzzing in the back of my head became an all-out scream. Meg's voice reverberated in my mind, her panic and fear a maelstrom atop the emotional tsunami threatening to obliterate me. I cinched our bond as tight as I could, until her voice and emotions faded into the background once more.

I peeled my eyelids open and forced myself to look at Hades, but in my mind, I saw Emi's vacant eyes. Raiden's. My mom's. I saw her slack face. The hole seared through her forehead. Her eyes. Her *dead* eyes.

How long until the light faded from Hades' eyes as well? How long until those crisp, ice-blue irises dulled to gray? How long until I made a mistake that cost *his life* as well? Considering what I had been planning to do, not long at all.

"You—you can't be here." Panic coiled around my ribcage, constricting until I could barely breathe, and I clutched at my chest. "You can't *be* here!" I shrieked.

I thought of him dying down here, caught in the middle of a fight *I* had picked versus opponents he stood zero chance of holding his own against. White-hot rage flickered to life in my chest, driving away the panic. I dragged in lungfuls of air, fueling the fire in my heart. In my blood.

"You *can't* be here," I ground out. And then I lunged at Hades.

He sidestepped at the last possible second, narrowly evading me.

I feinted right, and he moved with me.

"If you're determined to die down here," Hades hissed, dodging me yet again. "Then I'm going out with you."

My rage sputtered, then died out, and my heart seemed to sink into my stomach. Desperate, despondent, I shook my head. "The others on the ship—" I swallowed, nausea roiling in my gut. Whether it was nerves or the early onset of radiation sickness, it was impossible to say. "They don't need me, but they *do* need you. They won't make it, Hades. They won't *survive* without you."

The visible upper half of Hades' face contorted into something ferocious, and he lunged toward me, capturing my shoulders in an iron grip and pressing me back against a post. I was too stunned to resist. He leaned in until his face was mere inches from mine. "*I* won't survive without *you*, Cora," Hades professed, his voice ragged. "*I* need you."

Tears welled as I stared back at him, searching his furious glare. I had never seen him like this, so raw and volatile. I had never seen him lose his grip on his emotions completely, not even when I had been dying in his arms all those millennia ago.

Hades' grip on my arms turned painful, even through the protection of my hoplon suit, and he shook me. "It was never about them," he said, his voice low and tremulous. "It was never about our people—about bringing them back. From the moment you died, everything I did was only ever about you. About bringing *you* back." His throat bobbed, and he added more quietly, "About bringing you back *to me*."

I recalled the words he had spoken at the Alpha site shortly before we left Earth, what felt like a lifetime ago. I had asked him why he hadn't been able to let me go.

I couldn't. I had nothing left. Nothing to look forward to. Nothing to keep me going. To let you go would have been to give up, and I—I just couldn't. I couldn't do it.

I had accused him of dangling the promise of my resurrection in front of himself like a carrot. But what if it was more than that? Not merely a reward but a requirement.

Tears spilled over the brims of my eyelids, my chest heaving.

"I have no problem dangling the survival of our people," Hades seethed quietly, leaning ever closer, "the survival of your mom and everyone else you love in front of you to get you back on that ship." He was so close now that I could see the iridescent flecks icing his blue irises. "We can all live, or we can all die, but I refuse to suffer through existence without you again."

I searched his gaze, reading nothing but conviction. Hades would die with me. He was ready.

Hades released me, and I took a step back, rubbing my sore arm with my free hand. He watched me warily, like he still expected me to attack him. "What happens next," he said, "is entirely up to you."

I gritted my teeth, my nostrils flaring behind my mask as I inhaled and exhaled. Again. *Again.* On my next inhale, I opened my mouth, intending to admit defeat and tell him I would return to the *Elysium* with him.

A whisper of a sound snagged my attention, and I jerked my head around sharply. The unspoken surrender lodged in my throat, and I held up a hand, silently telling Hades to be quiet.

I heard it again a few seconds later—the scuff of a stealthy footstep. Then another, from the opposite direction. I glanced at Hades, only to find his eyes opened wide with alarm. He heard it, too.

The Titans had arrived.

23

THE TITANS HAD REACHED the amphitheater, lured by my bait. My plan had worked perfectly, aside from one massive snag.

I locked stares with Hades and gritted my teeth.

Hades showing up left me with two options. I could either drag him back to my hiding spot among the rubble and ash, hoping none of the Titans caught us while we snuck through the eerily glowing corridor. We would have to huddle together as we waited until the Titans were within the arena, then detonate the trap and run like hell to get out of range of the EM grenades.

The problem with that option was that I wasn't certain I could deactivate my regulator and put up a solid enough shield in time to protect Hades from the plasma blast. Once it was flush with psychic energy, my hoplon suit would protect me, but Hades' armor wouldn't stand a chance. I would be trading his life for the resources the *Elysium* so desperately needed.

Or we could flee while the Titans were distracted by that big, tasty ball of psychic energy I had left out to lure them in. The *Elysium* would still be dangerously low on Technetium, but at least we would both be far more likely to survive. *Hades* would be far more likely to survive.

Like there was even a choice.

I pointed with my chin toward the glowing green vines forming a curtain between us and the exterior corridor and touched a single, extended finger to the front of my mask, then held up my hands, palms out. *That way*, I told him with my body. *Quiet. Slow.*

Hades nodded once, telling me he comprehended my meaning. I sure as hell hoped so because he hadn't been remotely stealthy when he had been searching for me.

I held Hades' stare, willing him to understand that he needed to be sneakier than before.

Again, he nodded.

Pursing my lips, I turned my attention to the glowing green curtain of fungus. I could feel more than hear Meg in the very back recesses of my mind, eager to help. I sent a silent plea for her to remain as calm as possible; any distracting thoughts or emotions that leaked through our bond from her to me could be deadly right now.

My heart lodged in my throat as I inched closer to the curtain of fungus, pausing at the irradiated barrier.

A Titan passed by, mere feet away.

Breath held, I counted ten heartbeats before I could no longer see the Titan through my narrow vantage point. I exhaled, slow and controlled, and counted ten more.

And then I pushed through the thick, fuzzy living curtain and hesitated on the threshold between corridors. I glanced to one side, then the other. No Titans in sight.

I waved Hades forward, and together, we snuck across the corridor. We paused for the briefest moment at the next curtain of fungus. I peeked through the gaps between fuzzy, hanging vines and didn't spot any movement. A mid-sized tower in far better condition than the arena filled the block across the street.

Again, I waved Hades forward, and we crept out into the open street. We ducked into the ground floor of the neighboring building and raced to the far side, only slowing when we reached the exterior wall. We crossed another street undetected and slipped into the precariously leaning skyscraper I had noticed on my way to the amphitheater.

The ground rumbled suddenly, then shook hard enough to knock us both into one of the decaying building's inner walls.

The Titans had detonated my trap. They must have been trying to dismantle it and accidentally set it off instead.

The wall crumbled on contact, and Hades and I instinctively gripped glowing green vines for stability. A jolt of psychic energy zipped up my arm, and I reflexively released the vine and staggered to the side. Hades caught my arm, steadying me as the ground continued to quake.

The shaking had barely stopped when the building towering dozens of floors overhead groaned, then crackled like the slow shattering of tempered glass. Hades and I both looked up. It was, quite possibly, the most terrifying sound I had ever heard.

I grabbed Hades' arm and dragged him across the ground floor of the collapsing skyscraper. Massive chunks of the rotting building rained down on us, the first sprinklings of the death that awaited us should we linger.

Forgoing any pretense of stealth, we bolted through an opening in the nearest exterior wall. We hightailed it up the street, taking sharp turns whenever a bordering building wavered, heading vaguely in the right direction of the part of the city where I had parked the *Argo*.

Without warning, a shimmering barrier of acid-green energy erupted from the ground half a block away. It curved inward as it reached up, up, up, forming a dome high overhead. To maintain such an enormous field of psychic energy for more than a few seconds, they would have had to tap into the virtually bottomless well of energy stored within the fungus.

Hades and I skittered to a stop and stared at the wall of psychic energy. There would be no way for me to break through it, even if I deactivated my regulator and unleashed a blast from my doru with a fully charged focus crystal. This barrier had been created by multiple Titans, drawing on an endless fuel source. I was *far* outmatched.

I turned, staring at the far side of the dome, at least a mile away. A few towers remained, standing tall among the collapsed ruins of the other buildings.

We were trapped. With the Titans, no less. There was no way out.

We were trapped.

I thought my heart might explode from the overload of fear. I had never felt anything like this before. The terror was crippling. All-consuming.

Hades grabbed my arm and pulled me into the safety of a stable building nearby.

Once we were inside, hidden and relatively safe—for the time being—I turned to Hades, needing to see him. Needing the visual reminder that, for the moment, he was all right.

Hades moved in close, bowing his head to bring his respirator closer to my ear. "My ship is nearby. We can hide out there until we figure out a way through that barrier. It won't make it back out through the atmosphere, but at least it will protect us from the Pasitheorales Viride and further exposure to the radiation, for the time being."

I nodded fervently. Without the walls blocking out my emotions, without the distance of my temporary dissociation, I could see how reckless my plan had been, and I wanted nothing more than to get the hell out of there.

Hades led the way to the far side of the building, then across two more streets and through another pair of squat, relatively stable structures. We crossed one more street, and when we entered the tall building on the far side, Hades surprised me by leading me to a descending stairwell.

"Your ship is underground?" I asked, my brows bunching together as we hurried down the stairs.

"The shuttle was damaged during entry, and the cloak was failing," Hades explained. "I had to find a hidden place to set down fast. Otherwise, I would have landed near the *Argo* and caught up with you earlier."

"I see," I murmured, choking on guilt about why and how he had ended up on the planet.

Silenced by my mounting shame, I followed Hades down into near absolute darkness, illuminated only by the fungus branching all over the floor, walls, and patchy ceiling of a cavernous basement. Hades' small shuttle sat in full view of any who happened to venture down here.

We slowed as we approached the ship, and I spotted a large opening in the ceiling near the far end of the basement, offering a peekaboo view of the shimmering green dome trapping us in this part of the city. I figured that hole in the ceiling must have been how Hades flew down here.

"We're covered in Pasitheorales Viride spores," Hades said, powering up his holoband to remotely open the exterior door to the ship's tiny airlock. "We'll need to strip down and send our armor and gear through the decontamination chamber."

I glanced down at myself, my eyebrows shooting up. I was glowing with that same eerie green luminescence as everything else in this place. I looked at Hades, but he only had a faint green sheen.

Hades swept his arm out for me to board first, and I raced up the steps and into the airlock compartment, lit only by a quartet of tiny, orange emergency lights tucked into the corners. I turned, backing all the way to the interior door, and waited for Hades to join me.

Hades climbed into the cramped space, then pushed the button to close the exterior door, sealing us in the dimly lit compartment.

Keeping my knees and elbows angled away from Hades, I hastily stripped down to my underwear and bandeau bra, crouching to tuck everything—hoplon suit, boots, respirator, and weapons—into the chute that fed into the decontamination chamber. Straightening, I sidestepped so Hades could add his things to the chute.

My gaze caught on his bared shoulders and back. On all that lean muscle and pale, almost incandescent skin. On the intricate design covering almost his entire back in black ink. And on the scars crisscrossing the lines of the tattoo. I had never seen so much of him—never would have guessed the tattoos were even there, hidden under his clothing—and I couldn't look away.

I leaned in closer, studying the design inked into his skin in the dim lighting. Not merely a design, I realized. A *map*.

"Hand me your hood," Hades murmured, glancing over his shoulder at me. "And your comms patch."

I jerked back and dragged my stare up to his face, trying really, *really* hard to keep my focus above his shoulders.

His attention skimmed over my body like he just couldn't help himself. The touch of his gaze lit me on fire from within.

I cleared my throat, my neck and cheeks heating. "We don't need the hoods?"

Hades' eyes flicked upward, meeting mine. Could he tell I was blushing? He shook his head. "The EM shield is still functional," he said, his voice lower and rougher than before. Wait—was *he* blushing? "You won't be able to use your gifts," he added. The corner of his mouth tensed and lifted infinitesimally. "But then, neither will they."

"All right," I said, nodding my understanding. I pushed the hood back, then unfastened the clasp at my neck and handed it to Hades, then peeled off my comms patch and handed him that, as well. In the back of my mind, I wondered if the comms patch had been how he had tracked me.

He stuffed both of our hoods into the chute, then stood, turning to face me as he straightened to his full, towering height.

More ink decorated the front of his body, the columns of Olympian symbols drawing my attention down to his torso and lower. The ink disappeared behind his boxer-brief style underwear, only to continue down the fronts of his thighs.

Hades cleared his throat, and my attention snapped up to his face. I tilted my head back, arching my neck. Hades leaned forward, extending an arm to reach around me.

Past me.

A faint buzz alerted us that the inner airlock door was about to open. Air hissed, and a decontamination mist sprayed from the walls and ceiling. The sanitizer stung my eyes, but I couldn't stop staring at Hades. My heart was suddenly pounding, my breaths coming too fast.

Behind me, the door panel whooshed open.

Hades inhaled deeply and clenched his jaw, anger simmering in his stare. His focus shifted past me to the ship's compact cabin.

Taking the hint, I lowered my focus to the floor and turned away, retreating into the ship.

24

THE SHUTTLE'S CABIN WAS compact, about an eighth the size of the *Argo*, illuminated only by the dim orange emergency lights scattered around the perimeter of the floor and the eerie green glow from the fungus visible through the viewscreen. Shivering, I crossed to the front of the ship and gripped the top of the pilot's seatback.

I listened to Hades' hushed footsteps as he moved around the cabin behind me, to the hiss of a compartment opening, then the click of it shutting again. My heart beat faster as the sound of his footsteps told me he was approaching. By the time he stopped, standing directly behind me, my heart thundered in my chest. Goose bumps rose, covering my skin.

"Here," Hades said, draping the thin, soft fabric of an emergency blanket over my shoulders. "We might as well get comfortable. We're going to be here for a while."

I gripped the corners of the blanket and wrapped it tightly around me, clutching it shut over my chest. "Thanks," I whispered, turning to face Hades.

He was already walking away, another blanket wrapped around his own shoulders, the ends fluttering behind him like a cloak as he retreated to the other side of the cabin.

"Hades?" I said, his name a question. A plea.

He stopped, but he didn't turn to face me.

"Why?" I asked, unsure of what exactly I was asking.

Hades peered over his shoulder, showing me his angular profile. He clenched his jaw but didn't say anything.

"Why did you come?" I asked, thinking out loud. "Of all the times I've risked my life, why chase after me *this time*?"

Hades angled his face away and bowed his head, but his shoulders remained stiff, his back ramrod straight. "Because all the other times, I knew you would fight to get back to me," he said. "But not this time. *This time* was different. I could see it in your eyes—that you felt like you had nothing left to lose, and if I didn't follow you, I would never see you again."

I took a step toward Hades, drawn in by the emotion lacing his words. "You would have seen me in the simulation," I said softly.

Once they had confirmed my death on *Othrys*, if I had indeed died, my backup consciousness would have been uploaded to the simulation, just as my mom, Emi, and Raiden likely already were. If I released the clamp on my bond with Meg, I would know for sure, but I wasn't ready to battle her emotions while mine were still so unwieldy.

"It's not the same," Hades bit out.

I paused, unused to seeing such raw emotion from him. Such vulnerability.

Hades took a deep breath. "You loved him; I know that," Hades said. "And after what happened in the dining room . . ." He fell quiet for a moment, as though struggling with the words. "You lost everything you loved, and now you have nothing left."

I shook my head, silently arguing with him. He had it all wrong. Losing them wasn't what drove me to withdraw. To flee. To pursue this reckless mission that was, at its heart, a desperate attempt to hold on to what mattered most to me.

"You're wrong," I blurted, taking another step toward Hades. Another.

"Am I?" Hades asked.

I continued my slow approach. "I wasn't running away from all of that," I told him. "I was running from you."

Hades barked a laugh, harsh and humorless, and finally turned to face me. I noted he had knotted his blanket around his neck to hold it in place. He crossed his arms over his chest and parted his lips, sucking in a breath to speak.

But I beat him to it. "I did love Raiden," I admitted. "I *do* love him."

Hades flinched with each statement, like I had slapped him.

I stopped just out of arm's reach of him. "But you, Hades—you're the one I can't lose," I said, my voice thick with emotion. My chin trembled, and my nostrils flared. I blinked, setting free a fresh string of tears gliding down either cheek. I inhaled shakily, then continued. "When I was up there, and they were all—" I choked on the word *dead*. Their bodies were dead, but *they* lived on. "When their bodies were all around me," I amended, "I realized something."

Again, Hades clenched and unclenched his jaw.

I balled my hands into fists, strengthening my resolve, then confessed the truth. "I would rather die so you can live than risk living on without you." I cringed, only now seeing how selfish I had been. I had been so mad at Raiden for doing that exact thing.

It seemed so obvious now why I had been keeping my distance from Hades. Why I hadn't let our relationship progress, despite both of us wanting it to. I was afraid.

With him, I had always been afraid because I knew—I *knew*—that loving him would ruin me. And I couldn't help but wonder if he had realized the same thing long ago. Had he been so patient with me, waited without pushing for so long—for literal lifetimes—because he felt the same? Because he knew we were the endgame? That when we finally came together, once and for all, there would only be one path forward—a path we walked together?

Hades stared at me with eyes opened wide, his lips parted like he wanted to say something but couldn't find the words.

"I just lost three of the people I love most in the whole universe," I said. "And yes, I know they're not really gone, but as you said—it's not the same. I'll live on in this body, in and out of cryosleep, during the rest of the journey to Terra, while they'll spend countless lifetimes in the simulation. They will grow and change, while *I* will remain the same. They will *move on* in their new world, in future versions of themselves, but I'll still be out here, stuck in the past."

Hades watched my face as I spoke, but he didn't interrupt.

I drew in a breath, preparing to confess the truth I had buried into the deepest, darkest part of my heart. "I can't stand the idea of that happening with you, too," I said, choking on the grief of something that hadn't even come to pass. "If I lost you—" I paused, picking my words carefully and enunciating clearly, "If I lost you, Hades, I would not survive."

"Cora," Hades said, my name sounding like it had been ripped from his throat. His chest and shoulders rose and fell with each exaggerated breath. His arms loosened and lowered. He started to reach for me.

I held up my hand to hold him off, clutching the blanket around my torso with the other. "I don't want to live without you, Hades," I professed, my voice raw and ragged. "I *refuse* to do it, and ensuring the *Elysium* had everything it needed to make the trip to Terra was the surest way to guarantee *that* never happened."

"By throwing your life away?" Hades said, his voice rising.

"I'm sorry!" I wailed. "I wasn't thinking straight, and *I'm sorry*." I covered my face with my free hand, hiding from him as shame consumed me.

Hades' fingers wrapped around my wrists, his grip firm but gentle, and he pulled my hands away. His gaze searched mine, shifting from one eye to the other, again and again. He released my wrists and pressed his palms to either side of my face. "I forgive you," he whispered.

I closed my eyes, overwhelmed by the devotion burning in his gaze. The love that had simmered across lifetimes. That had spanned millennia.

"There is nothing you could do that I wouldn't forgive," Hades said, his words a soft caress. His lips brushed against mine, the touch hesitant, like his kiss was a question.

I froze, and my eyelids flew open.

Hades pulled back a few inches but didn't lower his hands from my face. For long seconds, all we did was gaze at one another. For lifetimes, that was all we *had* done. It was time we moved past longing stares. Past time.

I grabbed the knot of fabric tied at Hades' neck and pulled him closer to me, crushing his lips against mine. All hesitancy vanished from Hades with this second kiss. His reserved, controlled veneer sloughed away, revealing the pure, carnal desire beneath, and we crashed into one another.

Hades ripped away the blanket I still clutched in one hand, tossing it aside, while I tore at the knot tied around his neck. A second wave of goose bumps pebbled my skin at the sudden rush of cool air.

Hands bracketing my ribcage, Hades walked me backward, our kiss never breaking. My back hit the wall of the ship just as I worked the knot around his neck free, and Hades' blanket dropped to the floor. I pushed down my underwear, shimmying my hips and legs until the undergarment dropped as well, then kicked the scrap of fabric away.

Hades' hands slid down over my waist and the curve of my hips, then lower. He gripped the backs of my thighs, and I locked my arms around his neck, holding on tight as he lifted my feet off the floor. I wrapped my legs around his hips, hooking my ankles behind him, and gasped as he entered me.

And not once did we break the kiss.

We moved together, devolving to base creatures driven solely by the urgent need to be one. To belong to one another. To finally—*finally*—accept the inevitability of *us*.

Whatever lies I told myself before, it had always been him. It would always be him.

The ancient Olympians believed souls had been split in half and that the purpose of living was to find our missing piece. Our other half. We had long ago discounted their superstitions and religious beliefs. But right now, right here, with my body joined with Hades and nirvana spreading out from the core of my being, I couldn't help but wonder if they had been right all along.

25

I LAID ON MY side on the floor of the ship with my head resting on Hades' shoulder and my hand splayed on his chest over his heart. Hades was stretched out on his back beside me, one arm curled around my ribcage, the other folded and tucked behind his head to use as a pillow. His fingertips danced lightly over my skin, making my nerve endings tingle. The thin emergency blankets were all that separated us from the cold, hard metal floor. It was far from comfortable, but I hardly cared.

Not when we were here, trapped together until the Titans dispelled the dome of psychic energy surrounding this part of the ruined city, which wasn't likely to happen anytime soon. They knew another psychic was here, somewhere, hiding from them. They had all the advantages—time, numbers, resources. They could maintain that stupid dome indefinitely or until they found our hiding spot. Not that they were the only enemy we had to contend with. The shuttle would shield us from further exposure to the radiation, but we had already been out there for long enough to soak up a lethal dose if left untended. Soon, we would feel the effects.

I trembled, my body tense with the effort to hold in silent sobs. Tears leaked from my eyes, trailing across my temple and pooling against the bridge of my nose. I had tried so hard not to cry, but I had failed miserably. Now, my only hope was that Hades didn't notice.

But even as I thought that, Hades stiffened, his abdominal muscles flexing, and I held my breath. He pressed gentle fingers under my jaw, angling my face up toward his, and peered down at me, his head raised from the floor.

His gaze trailed over my face, lingering on my tears, and his expression turned somber. "We were in a state of heightened adrenaline, so I understand if you regret what happened," he said, his voice quiet and controlled. Too controlled.

I expelled my held breath in a laugh, then sniffled. "You're an idiot."

Hades frowned, his eyelids narrowing. "You *don't* regret what happened?"

Chin resting on his shoulder, I shook my head. I regretted so many things, but not that.

Relief relaxed Hades' expression, and he brushed away my tears with the pad of his thumb. "What is it, then?" he asked, his eyes searching mine. "Is it about your mom and—" He seemed to catch himself before saying Raiden's name. "And what happened up there?"

Sighing, I turned my head, once again resting my cheek on his shoulder. "That's part of it," I murmured. I traced the lines of text inked into his sternum—this portion written in Egyptian hieroglyphs—as I gathered my thoughts.

"If it is any comfort, I'm certain Fiona would have uploaded all who fell during the attack to the simulation by now, and—" Hades inhaled, then hesitated.

I raised my head to peer up at his face.

"I've gone over it again and again in my head," he finally said, "and I think Raiden was a mimic." When I frowned, he added, "A Tsakali clone with a pre-programmed, usually brief shelf life."

I shook my head, my brows bunching together. "I've never heard of them."

"They're an ancient tech," Hades said, resting his head back on his folded arm. "Almost impossible to detect due to the manner of their creation."

I raised my eyebrows, curious what he meant.

"They are essentially a perfect replica—an exact organic copy, fully formed, of the original at the time of the mimic's making. Everything would have looked and felt like the real Raiden—pheromones, scars, brain structure . . ." Again, Hades hesitated, glancing at me, then back up at the ceiling. "But the original would have been destroyed in the duplication process."

My chin trembled, and tears welled anew. I closed my eyes and turned my face away from Hades, once again resting my head on his shoulder. If he was right, then Raiden *had* actually been captured and killed by the Tsakali.

"Is it painful?" I asked, my voice a hushed squeak.

"No," Hades said definitively. "And for what it's worth, while the Tsakali are very cold and calculating in their pursuit of chaos energy, they are never cruel for cruelty's sake. Their synthetic natures render them no longer capable of such a thing. They would have created the mimic as soon as they captured Raiden, then planted it on Othrys, bait and trap."

"I see," I said quietly. Had they hoped to take down the entire ship with the mimic alone? Or had they planned on the Titans sneaking on board as well? Any way I looked at it, it seemed like a flimsy plan for such a *cold and calculating* enemy.

"I hope you can find some comfort in that," Hades said, his body tensing like he had again raised his head to peer down at me. "Though now that I've said it out loud, I can see how it may be more disturbing than I had intended."

A dozen heartbeats passed as I considered this revelation. Another dozen as I processed what it meant for Raiden and how terrifying his final moments of life must have been. Another dozen as I waited for a swell of despair. Of grief. Of agony. But all that came was a strange sense of peace, knowing it hadn't been him. *My* Raiden hadn't pulled the trigger. Hadn't killed my mom. Hadn't almost killed me, as well.

It was over. The hunt for Raiden had come to a conclusion. He had died, and I had been duped. But then, so had Emi.

My heart hurt when I thought of Emi and all she must have been going through with the mimic, trying and failing to rekindle some spark of humanity—of Raiden—in *that creature*. Not for the first time, I considered it a blessing that she had injured her brain with the blast from the laser pistol. Fiona would have been forced to upload Emi's stored, backup consciousness to the simulation. The version of her that would live on would have no memory of the recent, disturbing events. The same went for my mom and Raiden.

"That does help," I finally said, and some of the tension eased from Hades' body.

Now that my temporary psychotic break was in the past and my rational mind had prevailed, I was able to find reassurance in the knowledge that my mom, Emi, and Raiden—the real Raiden, not the mimic—were already safely ensconced in the simulation. Even with the bond between us clamped tightly, I could glean that much from Meg's mind, along with sickening threads of her panic and fear that leaked through.

"I just—" I inhaled deeply, exhaling another sigh. "I wish we had more time." I laughed bitterly. "I wish I hadn't wasted literal lifetimes running from this. From us."

Hades' arm tightened around me. "We found our way to each other eventually."

Another humorless laugh shook my chest. "And now what? We'll have a few days together until they find us . . . or until the radiation kills us." Frustration simmered within me. "I can't see any way out of this."

Through our bond, I sensed Meg champing at the bit to get down to the surface with every psychic on the *Elysium* backing her up. At that exact moment, a team was working to repair another shuttle to carry them on a rescue mission.

"Absolutely not!" I ordered silently, then cinched the clamp around our bond even tighter, seeking what privacy I could get.

"I can see a dozen ways out," Hades said, his voice resigned, "but none with the equipment and materials we currently have on hand."

I arched my neck so I could see his face. For long seconds, I watched him stare up at the ceiling of the ship, his focus shifting endlessly as the gears in his mind spun. "What would we need?" I asked, grasping at straws. Maybe we could find something down here, hidden in the ruins, and MacGyver our way out. Maybe there was still a way to survive this.

A dry chuckle shook Hades' chest. "A chaos bomb, to start," he said. "I would love nothing more than to obliterate those creatures, but I'm not greedy. I would settle for an EM grenade to nullify a portion of the barrier so we could escape." He fell quiet.

Goose bumps trailed his fingertips as they skimmed along the side of my body.

"But wishing gets us nowhere," he went on. "It's better to face the reality of our situation. This is likely it for us. We must accept that, make the best of what time we have left together, and take comfort in the knowledge that we will soon be uploaded to the simulation . . . minus our most recent memories."

His words didn't sit well with me. I gritted my teeth, a fresh round of tears brewing. If we died down here—which was highly likely—the versions of ourselves that lived on would have no memory of any of this. For all I knew, our uploaded selves would continue on, endlessly dancing around the will-they-won't-they situation, never fully realizing how much they mean to one another.

This wouldn't be the first time Hades and I died together. Our team had been trapped on a planet entering the event horizon of a black hole, and the gravitational disruption had prevented the gephyra from reconnecting. Our backup consciousnesses had been implanted into fresh bodies, left to speculate about what had happened to our previous counterparts after they crossed the gephyra bridge.

Hades' fingertips skimmed down the length of my arm, making me shiver. He threaded his fingers between mine and lifted my hand to his mouth, gliding his lips across my knuckles.

"Do you remember the Krystallos mission?" I asked quietly as Hades rested our joined hands on his chest, over his heart.

Hades' eyes locked with mine, and something in his stare made me think he already knew where I was going with this train of thought. "Of course," was all he said.

"Do you ever wonder if—" I hesitated, the question catching in my throat. "If, maybe, we found our way together, then?"

Hades' throat bobbed. "All the time," he said, his voice rougher than before. He blinked, and a tear leaked from the corner of his eye.

I raised my head, transfixed by the droplet as it streaked across his temple then vanished in his silken, silver-blond hair. "I'm sorry," I said, my voice barely audible. I had been the one holding back. For lifetimes, my fear had kept us apart. "I'm so, *so* sorry."

Hades closed his eyes and inhaled deeply, like he needed a moment to reel in his troubled emotions and regain his composure.

I hated seeing him in pain. I hated knowing *I* had caused it, and I wanted nothing more than to drive it away. To push all thoughts of our past angst out of his mind so he could focus on the here and now. After all, without a future to look forward to, the present was all we had left.

I slid my calf over Hades' legs and dragged my body up until I sat, straddling his thighs. Leaning forward, I pressed my lips to his chest, tracing the lines of text long ago inked into his skin. The light was too dim to read the tiny symbols, but I could at least follow their general flow. The corners of my mouth lifted as I felt him harden against my belly.

Hades reached for me, his fingers tangling in my loose hair and curving around the back of my head. He tried to pull me higher, to draw my face up to his.

I tensed, resisting, and shook my head. Gaze locked with his, I gripped his wrists and pulled his hands free from my hair, and then I lowered my head again. Ever so slowly, I kissed my way down the length of his torso, tracing this or that line of text.

Hades' breaths grew shallower and shakier, and the next time I glanced up, I saw him gazing down at me with no hint of that lingering sadness. The what-ifs and regrets had fled from his mind. There was only anticipation now. Only desire.

I smiled to myself. I had succeeded in taking away the pain. I licked my lips. Now, to give him something far more enjoyable to replace it.

26

"DO YOU THINK THEY'LL be able to complete the mission without you physically on board the *Elysium*?" I asked Hades.

We sat beside one another in the twin pilot seats, shrouded in shadows, emergency blankets wrapped around us like robes. Hades lazily skimmed his fingertips back and forth over the lower half of my legs, which were stretched across the gap between our seats and propped up on his lap. We gazed out the windshield and through the eerie green glow filling the cavernous basement to the hole in the ceiling. To the collapsed wall beyond. To the neon-green barrier of psychic energy.

"The mission to Terra?" Hades asked, turning his head against his seat's headrest to gaze at me.

"Yeah." I glanced at him sidelong, noting his raised eyebrows. "As much faith as I have in our collective ability to problem solve," I said, the confession hurting my heart, "I honestly can't see our way out of this mess."

Once Meg perished, confirming our deaths down here, our backups would be uploaded to the simulation up on the *Elysium*. Hades would still be able to assist with the mission, but his involvement would be downgraded from leader to consultant. It would fall to Fiona, Selene, and the Zari Amazons to hunt down the Technetium and complete the journey to Terra.

Hades' chest shook with a silent, humorless laugh. "Honestly, I can't see a way out either." Sighing, he faced forward once more. "I *do* think they'll be able to complete the mission," he said, finally addressing my actual question. "Much as it pains me to admit that I am not, in fact, essential." He chuckled again, dry but not completely devoid of amusement this time. "Your Fiona might just be the finest apprentice I've ever had," he added. "If anyone can accomplish what I have failed to do, she is the one to do it."

I smiled at that, lazily shaking my head against the seatback. "If, by some miracle, we make it out of this alive and get back to the *Elysium*, promise me you'll call Fio your apprentice to her face." I suppressed a giggle, imagining her reaction. It would be priceless.

Through my cinched bond with Meg, I sensed her extreme objection to my fatalist train of thought. Hades wasn't so disturbed, however, the ghost of a smile curving his lips.

Silence settled around us once more, but I felt antsy. I bent my leg, nudged the blanket aside, and skimmed the tips of my toes across Hades' abdomen, over the firm muscle and ink-stained skin, appreciating the way his abs tensed under my touch. This low on his torso, the text of the tattoo appeared to have been written in ancient Greek, though I couldn't say more in the dim light. Three long scars cut through the lines of text, clearly made by something with claws.

"How'd you get this scar?" I asked, tapping the middle line of the trio with my big toe.

Hades frowned and glanced down, then laughed hollowly. "I ventured too close to the den of a wolf with young pups while traveling through Macedonia," he said, letting his head fall back.

He was referring to one of the countless journeys he made while traveling around the world to monitor the progress of human civilization and set up his labyrinths, paving the way for my return to the land of the living. I couldn't imagine how lonely that must have been. I had read his logs, had felt his increasing desperation and despondency. If my thoughts had ventured into such depressing territory, I had little doubt that Hades' had as well.

"What's all this?" I asked, skimming my toes lower on his abdomen, over the lines of text inked into his skin beneath the scars.

Hades glanced down at himself once more, at my toes tracing lightly over his sensitive skin. I felt him harden against my ankle. He gripped my foot, stilling it, and gazed at me, heat simmering in his ice-blue irises. "Instructions for how to find the Omega site," he said, his voice rougher than before. "A failsafe during my travels long ago." His hand slid up my calf, his touch tickling the back of my knee, then higher. "But I don't want to talk about that."

I sucked in a breath when he reached mid-thigh, the light dance of his fingertips setting my nerve endings on fire. "What do you want to talk about?" I asked, the words noticeably shaky.

Hades' other hand glided up the inside of my neglected leg, and he scooted to the edge of his seat, then slid off to kneel on the floor. "I don't want to talk at all," he said as he pushed my legs apart. His focus dropped to the crux of my thighs, his expression turning worshipful.

I combed my fingers through his silver-blond hair as he moved closer, shouldering my legs further apart. With bated breath, I stared down at him, utterly transfixed. He inched closer. Closer still.

He stopped near enough for his exhaled breaths to caress me.

I sighed, letting my head fall back against the seat.

Hades chuckled, the sound like an electric shock to the very core of my being. And for a little while, at least, neither of us thought about the past. There was only the present. There were only the two of us, together.

27

I STOOD AT THE front of the shuttle, my hip leaning against the left-most portion of the control panel and my arms crossed over my chest as I stared out through the hole in the ceiling at the shimmering barrier of acid-green psychic energy. Hades kneeled on the floor in the back end of the ship, rummaging through the emergency supplies to see if any of the ancient, preserved food was salvageable.

I wasn't holding out hope for anything more substantial than a lackluster meal of stale water with a side of stale water. It wouldn't do much for our grumbling stomachs, but it would keep us alive a little longer, giving that much more time for radiation sickness to kick in or for the Titans to find us and kill us themselves.

My mood soured by the minute. I glanced over my shoulder at Hades.

Once again, he wore the Gargarean armor he had taken from the *Elysium*. I, too, had donned my hoplon suit. It was too cold to be lounging around nude any longer, as much fun as that had been. The temperature had steadily dropped as we pressed deeper into the night, and my breath faintly misted the air on every exhale.

I hated what we were doing—waiting to die. Accepting this end. This defeat. I chewed on my thumbnail, staring at the shimmering barrier trapping us here, and thought through any and every possible way to tear it down.

I figured I could probably make a hole in the barrier for a second or two—long enough for one of us to get through. But channeling psychic energy would give away my precise location. Besides, Hades would never leave me behind, and I would never leave him.

I wondered if there was a way to jury-rig an EM grenade. It would easily bust a hole in the barrier, and the lingering electromagnetism would keep it open plenty long enough for both of us to slip through. But Hades had already expressed his wish for an EM grenade. If we had the required materials to make one, he would have already started constructing it.

A dangerous thought whispered through my mind. I had channeled energy from the fungus before. If I had done it once, surely I could do it again. I could feel the energy pulsing through the veins of fungus every time I touched it. Not that it would make much of a difference when there were eight Titans and only one of me. I dismissed the idea.

Hades had mentioned a chaos bomb earlier, when we had been day-dreaming about finding a way out of this. I glanced down at my regula-tor, concealed in the protective golden orichalcum clamshell case. Selene had said the stone in a regulator was essentially a weak chaos fragment. A ludicrous idea popped into my head, and I curled my fingers around the case, capturing the concealed regulator in my fist.

"Hades?" I said, again looking toward the back of the ship.

He kneeled with his back to me, his head bowed as he sorted through the ancient supplies spread out on the floor around the emergency compartment. He sat up straighter and glanced at me over his shoulder. I couldn't make out his expression in the dim green glow. His face was a play of shadows of varying depths and darkness.

I hesitated only for a moment before asking, "How is a chaos bomb made?"

Hades grunted a guffaw. "Still searching for a way out?"

"Always," I said, attempting bravado, but it felt hollow. "I—" I licked my lips, then inhaled deeply. "I had a thought." Again, I hesitated. "A thought that might be completely ridiculous but also might *not* be."

Hades turned on the floor to face me, his armor creaking as he drew up one knee and propped an elbow atop it. "I'm listening."

"I just—" I gripped the regulator case tighter. "I need to know how a chaos bomb is made," I said. "If I'm right, there may be a way out of this for us after all."

Hades was quiet for a long moment, studying me like he was trying to read my mind to understand the direction of my thoughts. "A chaos bomb is created by repurposing nearly spent chaos fragments into an explosive device," he finally said. "The circuitry within the device creates a feedback loop that overloads the chaos fragments with external energy until they destabilize. The resulting explosion is absolutely devastating."

I nodded as he spoke, hope rising within me. Maybe this *could* work.

Hades stood and crossed the ship to join me. As the shadows thinned, I could see that his focus had shifted to my hand, his thoughts likely tracking mine to the regulator concealed within the cage of my fingers.

"I know what you're thinking," Hades said, stopping in front of me.

"That's usually my line," I teased half-heartedly.

Hades' focus shifted up to my face, and his eyes searched mine.

"Would the stone in my regulator explode like a chaos bomb if it were overloaded with external energy?" I asked.

Hades' expression tensed. "I believe so, yes."

"I thought so," I said, nodding to myself.

"The difficulty would be in overloading the stone," Hades said.

I pressed my lips together, already having devised a solution to that problem but anticipating that Hades wouldn't like it. "What if *I* over-loaded the stone with psychic energy?"

Hades sucked in a breath to argue.

I held up a hand, pressing my palm against his armored chest, and continued before he could start speaking. "I don't need to be close to the regulator," I said. "I just need a clean line of sight." I could channel psychic energy across miles, if need be, so long as I could *see* my target.

"They'll sense you the moment you start channeling," Hades countered. "They will know your exact location."

The corner of my mouth tensed. "How long would it take me to overload the stone?"

"That's impossible to say," Hades snapped.

"Guess," I demanded.

Hades inhaled deeply, his eyes remaining locked with mine. Finally, he let out a long, weary sigh. "A couple of minutes," he said, and it was as though the words were being dragged out of him.

I had been hoping for the overload time to be quicker, but I had been expecting the opposite.

"All right," I said, nodding to myself. It wasn't ideal, but it was man-ageable. I took a deep breath. "I have a plan," I told Hades, the corners of my mouth curving upward. "Nobody is killing us today."

There was still a good chance we would die, but at least we would go out in a blaze of glory. And, even better, we might just manage to take the Titans out with us.

28

I PUSHED THE BUTTON to open the inner airlock door and waited. Hades stood behind me, his presence wrapping around me like a cloak. A quiet alarm buzzed before the door panel slid to the side, and I stepped into the airlock compartment, moving to the far end of the cramped space so Hades could join me. I turned partway, watching as he ducked his head to enter.

"I remain uncertain of this plan," he said, punching the button on the control pad. The door panel slid shut, and a moment later, air hissed as the room sealed. Hades turned around to face me.

"It's our *only* way out of this," I reminded him, raising my eyebrows for emphasis.

Hades pressed his lips together into a thin, flat line.

"I *know* it's risky," I said, facing him fully. "But what other choice do we have?" I laughed quietly, the sound edged with bitterness. "Would you rather we simply lie down and wait to die?"

"Of course not," Hades snipped. He clenched his jaw and closed his eyes as though it pained him to look at me.

My ire dissipated, and I moved closer to him, studying the sharp angles and familiar lines of his face. I raised one hand and pressed my palm to his cheek. He leaned into my touch as I traced the line of his angular cheekbone with the pad of my thumb.

"I hate that you're here," I murmured. "That this plan risks your life, too." And Meg's life, back on the ship. I hadn't even considered her when I fled the *Elysium*, my mind warped by the fugue fueled by grief and desperation, and guilt over endangering her was slowly eating away at me. My chin threatened to tremble, and I refocused on Hades. "But I'm glad we're in this together."

Hades turned his face toward my palm, pressing a kiss to the heel of my hand. "There is no other person I would rather have with me at the end." He finally opened his eyes and looked at me.

My lips curved into a half-smile. "Same," I whispered, suddenly choking on the swell of emotion. I swallowed roughly, then cleared my throat, needing to tell Hades how I felt about him. Needing him to know I loved him desperately. "Hades, I—"

"Don't," he commanded, and the unspoken declaration lodged in my throat. "Not now. Not when you think we're going to die."

I pressed my lips together and nodded once, then flashed him a tremulous smile. "We should go," I said, lowering my hand and glancing over my shoulder to the exterior airlock door behind me.

Hades lowered his chin in affirmation, then raised his hood and lifted his respirator to cover his nose and mouth.

I did the same before turning to press the button on the control pad. The door panel slid open, and I jumped down to the basement floor, sending up a plume of irradiated spores all around me. I stepped to the side, waiting for Hades to join me and seal the shuttle.

"Did you have a location in mind?" Hades asked, turning toward me.

"I do," I said as I started toward the stairwell that had brought us down here. I heard his footsteps as he followed behind me. "It's close," I said, picturing a pair of skyscrapers I had spotted on opposite sides of the dome imprisoning us, both slicing through the upper part of the energy barrier.

The towers had been stable enough not to fall during the explosion in the amphitheater. It stood to reason they could withstand a couple of people climbing up several dozen flights of stairs, as well. The climb was imperative. It would buy me the time I needed to overload the regulator stone.

I was betting the Titans would split up once I started channeling, some heading for the regulator stone, some heading for me. Hades had calculated the blast radius of a chaos bomb formed around a single regulator stone to reach somewhere between a quarter and a half of a mile. Which meant my goal was to detonate the makeshift chaos bomb while the Titans coming after me were still within range of the blast.

The nearer of the two skyscrapers was only a block away from our hideout, and we reached it without difficulty. The climb up the seemingly endless flights of stairs, however, was grueling, especially when our bodies were weak from a lack of food and perhaps an unwise expenditure of energy on *other* activities.

I was both disappointed and relieved when I rounded the corner and discovered that the stairwell from the twenty-sixth to the twenty-seventh floors had caved in on itself. I'd been planning on climbing all the way up until we reached the Titan's energy barrier and could go no further.

Panting, I squeezed my side with one hand in a fruitless attempt to alleviate the stitch and scanned the decaying, fungus-covered wreckage on the twenty-sixth floor. "This'll have to do," I told Hades, who huffed and puffed up the final few stairs behind me.

I picked my way across the floor. It was a relatively wide, open space, and the indiscernible rubble gave no hint of what this building's purpose may have been. Not that it really mattered. I headed for the exterior wall that my gut told me faced the other tower on the far side of the dome.

My sense of direction did not fail me. The wall itself was mostly missing; only a few nubs of glass worn smooth by the elements and dusted with ash suggested it had once consisted of floor-to-ceiling glass. Through the opening, I had a clear view of the tower where I would make my big—but hopefully not *last*—stand, backlit by the vibrant green glow of the energy barrier. I thought it seemed a little lighter out, like Acheron was on the rise, though it was impossible to tell from within the dome.

I stood near the ledge and surveyed the time-ravaged space. I needed to find a spot to hang the regulator that would make it visible from high in the opposite tower but not from the ground. I couldn't risk giving the Titans a clear view of the source of the chaos signature they were sensing.

Where psychic energy was concerned, line of sight was immensely important. So long as the Titans couldn't *see* the regulator, they wouldn't be able to telekinetically retrieve it. And I *needed* them to waste time climbing up those twenty-six flights of stairs.

Hades' footsteps crunched as he crossed the floor to join me.

I glanced over my shoulder at him, my eyebrows raised in a silent question.

"It's a good location," he said, nodding slowly as he looked around. "You chose well."

I snorted a laugh. "Of course, I did," I said, trying to lighten the somber mood. "I do everything well."

"Don't I know it," Hades said softly.

I stared after him as he skirted around a support post jutting up from the floor at an angle, a flush warming my body. My stare caught on the jagged end of the post. On the fuzzy, three-foot-long vine of glowing green fungus hanging down until it almost scraped the floor.

I hurried over to the post and tugged away the vine of fungus. It resisted more than I had expected, snapping like there was a stem hidden within the inches of fuzz. I tossed it aside and wiped the end of the post clean with my hands. My gloves came away glowing neon green like they had been coated in glow-in-the-dark paint.

"This is a reckless plan," Meg cautioned me in my mind, her voice pushing through the clamped bond. I had been able to feel her disapproval since the plan took root in my head, but this was the first fully formed thought of hers that had reached me.

"It's the *only* plan," I shot back.

"I don't like it," she grumbled. What she didn't say, though I could sense it clearly enough, was that she feared removing my regulator would break our connection.

After all, our psychic bond had been forged by pairing our regulators. It seemed more likely that the true bond existed between the devices rather than between us. I both shared her fear and hoped it was the case. Not because I wished to be free of her but because the bond linked our lives. If I died down here, up on the *Elysium,* her life would end as well. I wanted to spare her that ending.

"I'm sorry, Meg," I muttered as I raised my hands and fished my regulator chain out from the collar of my hoplon suit.

I took a deep breath, then another, preparing myself for the influx of sensory input once my psychic powers were unleashed, wild and completely unregulated. The orichalcum-laced hood would help, but everything on this planet was coated in that damned fungus. Psychic energy was all around me. It was under my feet, pulsing against the bottoms of my boots.

After a third deep breath, I pulled the necklace off over my head. I hung it, protective case and all, from the notched spike at the end of the broken post, then released the chain and took a step back.

An influx of psychic energy throbbed all around me, and I had to consciously fight the urge to reach out and reclaim my regulator. The energy beneath my feet stretched on and on and on, extending to everywhere the Pasitheorales Viride reached. It was like viewing infinity, like standing in the heart of the universe with a clear view of all of existence spreading out around me.

I squeezed my eyelids shut, breathing through the momentary overload. No wonder the Titans had been able to maintain that massive dome for so long. Their supply of psychic energy was *endless*.

I inhaled deeply and held the air in my lungs, focusing on the physical sensations of my body, using the real and tangible to block out the pushy energy from the fungus. Once I felt confident in the mental wall I had formed between myself and the enormous well of psychic energy, I opened my eyes again.

The orichalcum-laced hood definitely helped. At least I wasn't fending off input from Hades' mind, as well as the pushy thrum of psychic energy beneath my feet.

Meg was still there, tucked into the corner of my mind reserved just for her. Relief poured into me through our bond, and I smiled to myself, just for a moment. There was our answer. Pairing our regulators may have initially formed our bond, but now it was our own. Now it was real. My smile wilted. I just wished my death wouldn't mean hers as well.

"The beacon is in place on the chain," Hades said, resting a hand on my shoulder. "We should go." Ghosts of his emotions whispered through my mind, carried through the link forged by his touch. I sensed his fear and regret, pride and love, and just a hint of his uncertainty. Not about the plan with the regulator.

About me. About my feelings for him. Even now, even if we survived this, he feared he would lose me. Insecurity *I* had fostered within him from lifetimes of holding back simmered, whispering doubts through his mind. Into his heart.

I turned to face him, covering his hand with mine. I curled my fingers around his armored glove and searched his gaze, looking for the shadows I had sensed within him.

Hades stared back, curiosity narrowing his eyes.

"I love you," I blurted, disregarding what he had said earlier. I *needed* him to know how I felt *now*. "I've loved you since I found you in that lab," I confessed.

I recalled finding him in his lab eons ago when the genetic coding equipment had "malfunctioned" thanks to some malicious tinkering by Poseidon. The losses to our people had been devastating, and none had been more distraught than Hades. It was the first time I had seen the depth of emotion concealed behind his frosty shell.

Hades stepped closer and bowed his neck, leaning in to rest his forehead against mine. "When you say such things, I am even less certain of this plan."

I smiled to myself behind my mask, hoping he could see it in my eyes. "I can live with that."

Panic poured through the bond I shared with Meg. My body tensed, and I hastily stepped backward, needing a clearer head than I could achieve with Hades' emotions clouding my mind.

"What's going on?" I asked her, easing up on the clamp on our bond to allow freer communication.

"Our chaos stone!" Meg practically shrieked. "It's gone!"

29

Lured in by Meg's panic, I closed my eyes and opened myself completely to the bond we shared, sinking into her mind. Through her ears, I heard the alarm blaring throughout the *Elysium*. Through her eyes, I saw women in hoplon suits rushing around her on the Bridge. Meg stood at the base of the stairs to the captain's platform, one foot on the lowest step, looking up. She watched Fiona at the top of the platform, frantically tapping and swiping at the holoscreen and uttering a string of foul obscenities.

It had happened mere moments ago. An alert popped up on the captain's holoscreen, immediately followed by the alarm. The chaos stone had been removed from its column. Gertie, the ship's AI, was powering down all non-essential systems.

My mind raced, rearranging the mismatching pieces of what I knew about everything that had happened since Raiden flew off in the decoy to lead the Tsakali away from the *Elysium*. My confusion over the attack by the Raiden mimic and what had seemed like such a foolhardy plan on the part of the Tsakali cleared. Was this their real goal all along—to steal our chaos stone? Had the Raiden mimic merely been the means to get a cloaked Titan on board the *Elysium* to steal it? The mimic's attack wasn't the plan—at least, not the whole plan. It was a distraction. For a *heist*.

"Lock down the ship!" I ordered through the bond.

Too late, as Fiona informed Meg of the external airlock door opening in the transport hangar.

Hades hovered near my right shoulder, and I pulled out of my deep dive into Meg's mind to relay to him what was happening on the *Elysium*.

"They must have taken one of our ships," he said, knowing Meg would hear him through our bond. "Otherwise, they would have used a side hatch to escape. It's likely a drop ship or a shuttle. Figure out which of our ships is active and track it."

Meg passed Hades' order on to Fiona, who swiped and tapped some more.

"The *Cerberus*," I relayed to Hades once Fiona shouted the name of the stolen shuttle to Meg. It was heading straight for Othrys.

"That makes sense," Hades said. "It was in the best shape of our remaining fleet of shuttles, but it needed repairs after recent use. It wasn't ready to withstand entry through a planet's atmosphere. Otherwise, I would have taken it myself." Hades paused. "The Titan must have waited for the mimic's distraction but missed her shot to take the only two shuttles capable of surviving the trip back down to Othrys. Her delay was likely due to the need to perform manual repairs on the shuttle."

I nodded, agreeing. "And now all of our people are stuck on the *Elysium*, not a single functioning ship available to chase after the chaos stone."

"It's headed straight for us," Hades reminded me. "We don't need to chase it."

I narrowed my eyes and set my jaw. We were the *Elysium's* only hope. "Then we had better get the hell out of here," I said.

"Good luck," Meg wished through the bond, necessity vaporizing all sense of her pessimism about my plan.

"Ready?" I asked Hades.

His chin dipped in a single, resolute nod.

As we hurried toward the stairwell—away from my regulator—I forced myself *not* to look back at the golden pendant. In this lifetime, the regulator had freed me. I had been a prisoner in my own body, held captive by my own mind. But from the moment my mom sent me the package with the regulator and I started wearing it around my neck, I had a new life. A *real* life outside of my cloistered existence on Orcas Island.

I rushed down the stairs. My leg muscles felt like jelly by the time I reached the bottom flight. I pressed onward, fueled by adrenaline and determination, only slowing when I reached the break in the curtain of fuzzy vines we had used as a door to enter the ground floor of the skyscraper.

Above us, the sky was on fire, Acheron burning on the horizon and heavy clouds roiling beyond the shimmering barrier of the dome. A streak of blinding lightning cut through the sky. A few seconds later, thunder rumbled.

"A storm is coming," Hades said from close behind me.

I almost laughed out loud. Could this situation be any more cliché? Of course, there would be thunder and lightning right before the boss battle. It would probably start raining, too. Could my life have been any more like a video game?

I reined in my mounting hysteria and glanced at Hades over my shoulder. "What are the odds that the rain here is acidic?" Another rumble of thunder.

"High," was Hades' only response as he stared out at the approaching storm. I suppressed the semi-hysterical laugh bubbling up from my chest. Of course. *Of course.* "The energy barrier will shield us," he said, then added, "while the dome still stands."

"Lucky us," I muttered.

More lightning streaked across the sky, thunder following soon after. I scanned the buildings visible from our position, then bolted across the street. I led the way through the contained portion of the city, darting into and out of the ground floors of the buildings that still stood. The storm was directly overhead by the time we reached the tower near the opposite edge of the dome. Thunder formed a near constant rumble, like a beast close on our heels.

I raced through the gaping doorway onto the ground floor of our target skyscraper and dashed around in search of the stairwell. Once I found it, I barreled up the stairs, legs straining and lungs burning. My heart pounded fast and hard, seeming to thump against the inside of my ribcage with each exaggerated beat. I blew past the tenth-floor landing, stumbled past the twentieth, and paused on the thirtieth, waiting for Hades to catch up.

"Should we keep going?" I asked Hades between heaving breaths as he finally appeared, feet dragging. It was less a matter of his physical fitness and more that his armor far outweighed mine. "Or do you think this is high enough?"

"The higher, the better," he said, gasping to catch his breath.

"Onward, then," I said before turning and darting up the next flight with renewed stamina. The burst of speed faded by the time I reached the thirty-first floor.

I stopped at the fortieth floor and bent over, hands on my knees. I still hadn't reached the green energy barrier, but there was a good chance I would puke if I kept going, which meant this would have to be high enough. Forty flights of stairs would *have to* buy us enough time for me to overload the regulator stone.

This floor was compartmentalized into hallways and smaller rooms, and it would have formed a labyrinth had the interior walls not crumbled long ago, replaced by curtains formed of fuzzy, faintly glowing vines. I pushed through "wall" after "wall," moving ever closer to the skyscraper's exterior. The growling thunder outside grew louder until, finally, I punched through one last shimmering green curtain, and it was a roar.

Like the skyscraper where we had left my regulator, this building's exterior wall was gone, discarded to the ground long ago, leaving fluffy vines of fungus as the only barrier between me and a forty-story drop. I inched closer to the edge and peered down, down, down. Shaking off the threat of vertigo, I focused on the distant tower, squinting and seeking a glint of blue from the beacon Hades had attached to the chain.

There!

I raised one hand, extended my arm out in front of me, and channeled psychic energy into a thin electric-blue thread, officially starting the clock. The Titans would be able to sense me now. Me and the psychic energy I channeled. They would be headed my way soon if they weren't already.

Breath held, I reached out with that electric-blue thread like it was an extension of my arm, guiding it across the distance stretching out between my current position and the regulator nearly a mile away. Farther and farther, I reached with that thread of psychic energy, straining to control the trajectory the longer it stretched.

Until finally, it connected, and I could breathe again.

I took a moment to relax my psychic fingers, then refocused on the thread connecting me to the regulator. I split the end of the thread into multiple strands and used them to carefully open the golden clamshell case shielding the regulator. Once it was open, I dropped the case to the floor and wrapped those strands of psychic energy around the dangling regulator pendant.

Hades' footsteps crunched through the debris littering the floor as he approached.

I angled my face toward him but didn't break focus with the blue beacon. "You're sure we'll be out of the blast zone?" I asked, my voice low and tense.

"Chaos explosions are extremely unpredictable," Hades murmured. "But I am as certain as I can be."

"All right," I said on my exhale. "Here we go."

I inhaled deeply, focusing on the regulator at the other end of the electric-blue tether, and drew from the psychic well within me. I gathered the energy in my outstretched hand until my arm was wreathed in crackling electric-blue lightning up to my elbow.

On my next exhale, I poured all of that gathered psychic energy into the thread stretching out between my hand and the regulator stone. The thread thickened, blazing visibly across the distance. I gritted my teeth, drawing more and more psychic energy out of my inner well and channeling the raging torrent into the regulator stone.

Time sped up. Stood still. Became irrelevant.

Sweat beaded on my brow and dripped down my forehead, and my breathing turned ragged. Rain showered from the sky, sizzling against the outside of the dome, and an acidic tang burned the back of my nose, even through the respirator.

Something shifted at the other end of the psychic tether. The anchor wobbled, loosening. My heart skipped a beat or three as I feared I was losing my grip on the stone. But the connection was strong. It was the stone itself that was weakening. Destabilizing.

I grinned behind my mask. "It's working!" I exclaimed, laughing and breathless. "It's *working*!"

Without warning, a rope of foreign psychic energy coiled around my tether, forming a noose that constricted until my torrent lessened to a trickle.

I gasped as the psychic energy I had been pouring through the tether recoiled back into me. Gritting my teeth, I focused everything within me on maintaining the connection.

"What is it?" Hades asked, hovering as close to my side as he could get without actually touching me.

"It's them—the Titans," I ground out. "They've found the regulator."

30

I GROUND MY TEETH together as I strained against the psychic chokehold the Titan had on my energy stream. I was *so close* to overloading the regulator stone. So close to detonating the makeshift chaos bomb. Just a few more seconds of channeling the full torrent of psychic energy into the stone, and it would blow.

The psychic bindings stretched, resisting. I groaned through the effort, clenching my hand into a fist, and pushed and pushed and *pushed*.

The noose released suddenly, and the breath whooshed from my lungs.

Panting as though I had just climbed up another forty flights of stairs, I redoubled my efforts, drawing more psychic energy from my inner well. I pushed the energy out through the tether connecting me to the increasingly unstable regulator stone. Almost there. *Almost . . .*

"NO!" I screamed as psychic energy began draining out of the regulator stone.

The Titan had redirected her efforts from attempting to block the flow into the regulator stone to siphoning energy from the stone. *My* psychic energy. She was likely absorbing it into herself, stabilizing the stone and refilling her own reserves of psychic energy at the same time.

She had the upper hand, drawing out the energy just a little faster than I could feed it in. The point of destabilization—of detonation—slid further and further away, and I was nearing the bottom of my psychic well.

I dropped to one knee, pushing onward. Straining to channel more, faster. But I knew. I *knew* it wouldn't work. Even if I could keep up with her at this point, if I could shove psychic energy into the stone faster than the Titan could draw it out, I didn't have enough left in me to detonate the stone.

Hades kneeled before me, off to the side enough that he didn't interfere with my waning stream of electric-blue energy. I was scraping the bottom of my well, pushing myself to the absolute limit. Much more, and I would risk psychic burnout—and likely death. Again. And with Hades kneeling there, I couldn't help but recall the last time I had died, when he had held me as I drew my last breath.

Hades caught me, pulling me onto his lap. He brushed the hair out of my face, his touch gentle, and stroked my cheek. The sensation remained long after my awareness of who he was or why he was touching me had faded away.

Grief and frustrations exploded out of me in a guttural cry. Olympians didn't believe in fate, but this scenario kept happening, and I couldn't help but wonder if my people had been wrong. Was this our destiny? Were we doomed to relive this star-crossed love and death cycle over and over again?

Tears leaked from the corners of my eyes as the tether thinned to a thread and the energy stream waned to a trickle. Even now, when defeat was all but certain, I couldn't let go. Couldn't break the connection. That regulator stone was our last hope. Our *only* hope to survive this together.

But Hades still had a chance. On his own, he could still make it out of here alive.

"You should go," I told Hades, my voice hoarse and tears streaking down my cheeks. "Hide. They'll already have a lock on my position, but for all they know, I'm alone up here. Once they've caught me, they'll drop the barrier. You can still make it out. You could still retrieve the chaos stone. This doesn't have to be the end for—"

Hades gripped my upper arms. His desperation and determination poured into me. "They won't just capture you, Cora," Hades said, his voice rough and urgent. "They will *destroy* you."

A whimper clawed up my throat and escaped from my lips. He felt *so much*. Pain and sorrow. But also love and hope. He still believed in me. He believed I would find a way through this, that we would *win*. His faith in me nearly broke me.

"But at least you'll survive," I sobbed. "At least one of us will remember what happened here."

Hades shook his head vehemently, and I sensed his resolve to stay with me. "Unacceptable," Hades declared, his voice rough and hard. "I refuse to go back to pretending you aren't the center of my universe."

I blinked, freeing a fresh string of tears.

"Either we leave this place together," Hades vowed. "Or not at all."

"I CAN'T DO IT!" I shouted. "I'm not strong enough," I added, my chest heaving with barely contained sobs. "*I'm* not enough."

"I won't leave you," Hades reiterated, his grip on my arms tightening, his resolve hardening. He meant it with every fiber of his being.

Hades *would not* leave me, which meant he would die here. We would both die here. And the next incarnations of us—if by some miracle the others on board the *Elysium* managed to recover the chaos stone and reach Terra, and there *was* a next incarnation of us—would never know all that had happened between us down here.

I trembled, barely holding myself together, and pushed back my hood. I felt claustrophobic in my armor. In my skin.

Lightheaded, I dropped my other knee to the floor and sat back on my heels. The Pasitheorales Viride hummed beneath me, making my shins tingle with pins and needles. It beckoned me, thrumming with vibrant energy. *Psychic* energy.

If I didn't do something *right now*, Hades was going to die.

My sobs abated, and I pressed my free hand to the floor. I dug my fingers into the carpet of fungus until my hand was covered almost to the wrist. I fed a few precious droplets of my natural psychic energy into the fungus, and it lapped the energy up greedily. The fuzzy, neon-green fungus crept up to my wrist.

I fed the fungus another trickle, sparing what little I could without breaking my connection to the regulator stone, and the fuzzy, neon-green film encasing my hand and wrist inched higher. It coated my entire forearm. Then it covered my elbow.

"What is this?" Hades gasped. He snatched his hand away when the creeping fungus nearly reached his armored glove. "What's happening?"

"It's all right," I told him, my voice strained. "Everything is going to be all right."

I fed the fungus one more little burst of psychic energy, ensuring my connection to it was as solid as it could be with such limited resources.

And then I reversed the flow, pulling, dragging, hauling the foreign energy into me. All around us, the veins of fungus lit up, glowing brighter, like fanned coals. I sat up straighter, strengthened by the sudden influx of psychic energy.

I sucked it into me, refilling my well until it overflowed, but I didn't stop there. Raising to my knees, I drew more energy from the fungus, channeling it directly out through my other hand and into the tether connecting me to the regulator stone.

Now that I had tapped into a free-flowing energy source, I could pour more psychic energy into the regulator stone faster than before, tipping the ratio of input to withdrawal in my favor. Energy flooded the regulator stone faster than the Titan could drain it, and once again, I clawed closer to the destabilization point.

"It's working," I said between heaving breaths. The sheer volume of energy flowing through me made my nerve endings sizzle. A roaring filled my ears, and I wasn't sure if it was the blood in my veins or the deluge of foreign psychic energy.

The drain on the stone increased in a sudden leap that could mean only one thing—another Titan had joined the first. I was still adding energy *slightly* faster than they could take it away, but not by much. At this rate, it would take hours to reach detonation, and we likely had minutes, at most, until the Titans reached us.

I had an idea. I would have one shot at this. One chance to trick them.

I slowed the flow of energy I was pushing across the tether, letting the Titans think I was running out of steam. Letting them think they had beaten me. But I didn't slow my draw on the fungus.

I opened my outstretched hand and turned it over, gathering the psychic energy in my palm, forming a writhing, aquamarine orb. I channeled more and more energy into my hand until streaks of electrified green lashed out from the dense ball, snapping and sizzling.

I was just about to unleash the gathered energy when I felt a tugging sensation deep inside me. My stomach dropped like I was in freefall, and I went momentarily breathless. And then it was like a hole had been drilled into the bottom of my inner psychic well, and the energy stored within was being sucked out through that hole.

I gasped, hunching my shoulders and bowing my spine. I couldn't catch my breath. The Titans weren't just draining the stone now. Somehow, they were also draining *me*.

Without my full concentration, energy slipped free of the orb in my hand, some flowing across the tether, some backflowing into me, replacing the energy the Titans were draining from my inner well. I shifted my focus from the stone at the other end of the tether to my psychic reservoir. I turned my attention inward, diving to the bottom of the well to patch the hole.

I found another tether there, connecting me to the Pasitheorales Viride. The fungus was one single organism, one vast network, a conduit of psychic energy stretching all over the planet. I followed my draining energy as it flowed out of me, pulled by a Titan through the veins of the fungus stretching to the tower at the far edge of the dome. Riding that current, I dove into the mind of the Titan attempting to drain me.

I blinked, momentarily disoriented by the shift in perspectives.

Through my psychic assailant's eyes, I could see that she stood near two other Titans, both with arms outstretched and a single fingertip each touching the regulator stone, though she wasn't touching it herself. A fourth Titan approached, having emerged from the stairwell. I sensed that two more were heading toward Hades and me at this very moment.

I could feel them through the fungus, racing across the ruins, closing in on this tower. It wouldn't be long until they were here, and I was already fighting two battles. I wouldn't be able to fend off a physical attack as well.

When the newcomer reached the Titan whose mind I had infiltrated, she placed her hand on my assailant's shoulder, linking their powers.

I gasped as the drain of energy from the hole in the bottom of my well more than doubled. The energy poured out of me, and I reeled in my consciousness, redoubling my effort to refill my reserves.

But I was no match for all four of the Titans—the two sucking energy from the regulator stone and the two draining my inner well. The piddly stream flowing across the tether to the regulator stone did little to offset what the Titans were siphoning away, and I had only managed to slow the drain within myself. I had thirty seconds, max, until my psychic well was drained dry. Until I burned out.

Until I died.

"I'm sorry," I squeaked to Hades. I was still staring across the distance to the other tower, stubbornly refusing to let go of the tether with the regulator stone. "I can't—" My heart lurched, skipping a beat. I dropped back down to sit on my heels. "I can't do it. There are too many of them. They've linked, and I just—I can't do it alone."

Hades wrapped his arms around me and tried to pull me in close, but I pushed him away with my elbow.

"They're coming!" I shrieked. "You have to go! Please, Hades. Leave me. *Leave me.*"

Hades tightened his hold on me, easily overcoming my weak efforts to resist as he pulled me in close. "Never," he hissed. "I will *never* leave you. I am with you until the end."

I sagged sideways against Hades and released a guttural sob.

"*As am I,*" another voice whispered through my mind, but I was too lost in grieving Hades' impending death to comprehend who had spoken those last words or what they meant.

I leaned against Hades, drawing in ragged breaths as the end hurtled ever closer.

It wouldn't be long now.

31

"**I**'M HERE, CORA," THAT voice whispered through my mind again. Was I imagining it?

"You're not alone." That voice—I knew that voice. It was in my head, but it was *real*. Meg. "I can help," she added. "We can link. But you have to *let me in*."

"I can't," I whimpered, speaking out loud. All my concentration was already split between maintaining the tether with the regulator stone and refilling my psychic well to delay the inevitable. It was as good as over now. All I had to do was to let go. It would be quicker than this slow, agonizing demise.

"Don't you dare!" Meg hissed.

I felt a tug within me, different from the Titans slurping the energy from my inner reservoir. This centered in my chest, a third tether, one that was stronger than the others. It stretched all the way through the planet's atmosphere to the *Elysium*, connecting me to Meg.

"If you die, I die," Meg reminded me, her mental voice urgent. "So *don't* die!" It was an order. A command. "Link with me, Cora. Let me in!"

I shook my head against Hades' shoulder. I was too exhausted—physically, mentally, emotionally, and psychically—to puzzle out what she wanted me to do. How could I *let her in* when she was already in my head?

"How?" I asked, my voice high and weak, laced with desperation.

"Release the clamp on our bond," Meg explained patiently, like we had all the time in the world. Like we weren't both about to die. "That's all you have to do. Just release the clamp, just let me in, and we can fight them together."

I inhaled a deep, shuddering breath, focused on the invisible cord spanning that vast distance between Meg and me, and relaxed my viselike grip. Meg's thoughts and emotions flowed freely into me, as I imagined mine flowed into her. I felt kind of bad about that. My heart and head were a mess.

The bond between us expanded, strengthening. I was drawn toward Meg, lured into her by the relative safety and comfort of the *Elysium*.

In a blink, I wasn't merely connected to her. I was *inside* her mind, her body. Her senses were my senses. Everything she saw, heard, and felt, *I* saw, heard, and felt.

I was on the Bridge, sitting on the floor, my back to the side of the navigation pedestal. My knees were drawn up in front of me, my elbows resting atop them, and my hands clasped together. Caly and Fiona kneeled side by side before me, twin expressions of concern tensing the corners of their mouths and furrowing their brows. Selene stood directly behind them, and dozens of Zari psychics crowded in around the trio.

The next generation of Amazons. Their solidarity warmed my heart, and I formed Meg's lips into the faintest smile.

Fiona's eyebrows rose.

Caly squinted as she watched me. "Cora?"

"Wait, what?" Fiona asked, glancing at Caly. "What the feck are you talking about?"

"I think Cora's here," the young psychic said, pointing to me—to Meg—with her chin.

Fiona's eyebrows climbed even higher.

Caly scooted closer to me until the side of her leg was flush against mine—against Meg's—and she leaned in, searching my—Meg's—eyes. I could feel her psychic senses reaching out to me. A tense, tight-lipped smile curved her lips, and she captured my—Meg's—hand, clasping it between both of hers. "It *is* you," she whispered.

"I have to get back," I said, but the voice that spoke my urgent words wasn't mine. "They're coming, and I can't leave Hades to face them alone."

"I agree," Caly said calmly. "You must return. But will you be going back to fight?" She hesitated for the briefest moment. A hard edge entered her voice when she added, "Or to die?"

I sensed something unexpected from Caly then. And from Meg, who had been momentarily displaced into *my* physical body but was still aware of what was going on in the *Elysium* with her own body. I felt a sense of fear from them both. Of desperation. Of loss born of love, or at least of the *possibility* of love. Their relationship had changed, becoming more. Hades' heart would be shattered by my death. Caly's heart would break, too over losing Meg.

"I want to live," I swore. I shook my—Meg's—head. "But I can't fight them. There are too many of them, and I'm not strong enough on my own."

Caly's grip on my hand tightened, and she bared her teeth in a ferocious smile. "As Meg already told you—" Psychic energy jolted up my—Meg's—arm as Caly linked with my temporary host body. "You are *not* alone. You have Meg, and you have me." Caly glanced around at the women crowding in behind her.

Selene and Melyse reached out to rest their hands on Caly's shoulders. Two more bursts of power zinged up my borrowed arm.

"You have *all of us*," Caly said.

The women beside and behind Selene and Melyse linked with them, adding their power to the psychic nexus. More Zari Amazons joined until over three dozen women had merged their powers. The force of it nearly brought me to tears.

I blinked, and the world blurred. Suddenly, I was back in my own body, leaning against Hades, the bond connecting me to Meg wide open.

It was then, when my sense of self reoriented to this place, to *my* body, that I felt it pouring into me through our bond. *More* than thoughts and emotions flowed into me from Meg. Psychic energy flooded into me from the nexus up on the *Elysium*, rushing through me, refilling my well far faster than the Titans could drain it. With it, my strength returned, and my will hardened to orichalcum.

I straightened, Hades helping me with a supportive hand above my elbow. Psychic energy charged my outstretched arm and erupted from my hand in a kaleidoscopic beam of every imaginable color. I channeled more psychic energy at one time than I ever had before, electrifying my very cells and setting my nerve endings on fire. I screamed as the collective force generated by our nexus roared through me and shot out of my hand, racing across the tether connecting me to the regulator stone.

In a matter of seconds, the regulator stone started to lose its stability. In the next heartbeat, hairline fissures formed in the once flawless stone, spider webbing out like a cracked windshield.

Hades released my arm and leapt to his feet, drawing his laser pistol. In my peripheral vision, I watched him fire a single blast before the regulator stone cracked.

And detonated.

The light reached us first, like a rainbow had exploded. I barely had time to blink before the shock wave hit, knocking me backward. I slammed into something hard, then rolled onto the lumpy rubble, grateful for the cushion of the fungus.

Groaning, I rolled onto my side, then onto my hands and knees. My ears rang, and my head spun. My thoughts were slippery and unformed. In my mind's eye, I held onto a single image—of Hades firing his laser pistol. I blinked and shook my head. The two Titans who had been heading our way must have finally arrived.

I raised my head and blinked again, trying *so hard* to focus. To *see*.

Crimson ash and irradiated spores clouded the air, filling this floor with a murky green haze. I spotted Hades' silver-blond hair nearby. He lay sprawled facedown on the floor, his laser pistol nowhere in sight.

Movement in my peripheral vision caught my eye, and I snapped my head to the right, my vision swimming.

There, a boot. A *Titan* boot. It shifted as the psychic wearing it bent her leg. Groaning, she propped herself up on her elbows. Her eyes narrowed when she spotted me watching her.

I froze, my breath lodging in my throat.

The Titan rolled onto her side with unexpected speed and shoved her arm out. Acid-green psychic energy crackled around her hand and forearm as she charged a killing blast.

But I was faster. Power surged through me from the nexus, and I raised my hand, releasing a multicolored ball of psychic energy. It struck her like a mini chaos blast, incinerating her on contact.

The world tilted and lurched. I feared this second explosion had been too much for our tower. Or had it just been too much for my body?

Darkness closed in all around me as my vision tunneled. My elbow buckled, and the lights of my consciousness winked out.

32

I CAME TO SLUNG over Hades' shoulder, bobbing with his unsteady gait. Meg was still there, in the back of my mind, but the link with the nexus had broken. Not that I minded. I felt like I had the mother of all hangovers.

I was never channeling that much psychic energy again.

Groaning, I raised my head to peer around. My hood had been drawn up over my hair, partially cutting off my range of vision. Fresh ash fell from the sky like snow, blanketing the ground and further obscuring what I could see.

Hades was carrying me down the middle of a street bordered by skeletal ruins coated in glowing green veins of the fungus. Even through the ash fall, I could tell that a few blocks back, the street abruptly gave way to the lip of a massive, smoldering crater. The result of the chaos explosion *I* had caused.

"Hades," I rasped, tapping on his lower back. "I'm awake. Put me down. Please."

Hades stopped, and his shoulder shifted uncomfortably against my abdomen as he lowered me to the ground. He set my feet down but maintained a steady hold on my waist as he peered into my eyes. "Are you sure you can walk?" he asked, his expression dubious.

Under the shadow of his raised hood, I searched what I could see of his face for injuries, but I found only a few scratches over his right eyebrow, deep enough that they would likely scar. I quickly scanned the rest of Hades, noting the blood leaking from a gouge in the armor on his thigh, just above his knee.

"It's not serious," Hades informed me when my stare lingered on his injured leg. "Merely painful."

I lifted my stare back up to meet his.

Hades released my waist and raised his hands, placing them gently on either side of my face. For a long moment, all we did was look at each other. We relished the fact that we still could. That we were *still alive.* That we had *survived.*

"I only saw one of the Titans when I woke," I said, hating to disrupt the moment. But it was necessary if we wanted to *keep on* surviving. "I took her out, but *two* were on their way to us."

"There were two," Hades said, nodding to himself. "The other must have been thrown from the building during the explosion," he said. "I saw her remains in the street on our way out."

I shifted my focus to his hood, then returned it to his eyes. "This is a precaution, then?" I asked.

"The chaos stone thief is still out there, somewhere," he reminded me, his hands falling away.

I closed my eyes, letting my head droop forward as my shoulders shook with something that was a hybrid between a laugh and a cry. "We're not done yet, are we?" I whined, then peered up at Hades without raising my head.

"Almost," he said. He turned partway and extended his arm, pointing up the street in the direction we had been headed. A thick plume of dark gray smoke rose from the ruins of a collapsed building about six blocks away.

"You think that's the thief's ship?" I asked, looking from the smoke plume to Hades and back. "You think she crashed there?"

Hades nodded and said, "Even with her hasty repairs, the *Cerberus* wasn't likely to survive entry through the atmosphere."

"I wonder if she knew," I thought aloud as I watched the rising smoke.

"What do you mean?" Hades asked.

"I wonder if she knew she would crash," I explained, shifting my focus back to Hades. "If she knew she wasn't likely to survive even before she left the *Elysium*."

From the way the skin tensed around Hades' eyes, I imagined a frown turning down the corners of his mouth behind his respirator. "She wouldn't have cared," he said. "There is no sense of self with the Tsakali. When they gave up their mortal bodies, they lost their individuality. All that remained was the whole."

I recalled the Titan who had teamed up with the pirates. She had definitely been her own person, so to speak. But then, she had been condemned to die by her own people for that same thing. Because she was different. Because she cared. Because she had what most humans would call *a soul*.

My shoulders slumped. "Let's get our chaos stone and get the hell out of here," I said, fighting off a wave of exhaustion.

"Gladly," Hades agreed, and we continued our way up the street, Hades limping slightly and my own feet dragging.

I blew out a breath. "I suppose we should grab the Technetium cartridges, too," I grumbled as we trudged onward.

I really wanted to get back to the *Elysium* and sleep for a few weeks. But the Titans were defeated. I hadn't sensed any others when I had been connected to the fungus. The Technetium cartridges and whatever else the Tsakali had stashed in their underground hideout were ours for the taking.

"We probably should," Hades agreed, sounding as unenthusiastic as I felt.

The corner of my mouth tensed. It was the closest thing to a smile I could manage at the moment, not that he could see it with my respirator blocking the lower half of my face. We would do it, obviously. We would retrieve the Technetium cartridges. But it warmed my heart to know Hades was as unenthused to extend our stay as I was, especially considering the telltale knot of nausea already twisting in my gut from prolonged exposure to the radiation.

We were about a quarter of a block away from the apparent crash site when I spotted movement in the shadows of the ruins emitting the smoke plume. I flung my arm out to the side, stopping Hades dead in his tracks, and reached over my shoulder to draw my doru. I extended the staff to its full length, gritting my teeth as energy sizzled along the singed psychic pathways within me. It felt like pouring alcohol on an open wound.

Pushing through the shocking pain, I charged the focus crystal atop my doru and aimed it at the shifting shadows.

A figure emerged, charred and stumbling. I assumed it was the remaining Titan, but she was unrecognizable as such. Her face was a blackened mess, her lower jaw missing and nothing but empty holes where her eyes should have been. I did, however, recognize the golden box she hugged to the front of her body. The chaos stone was in there, shielded by the containment cube's thick layers of orichalcum alloy.

On her next step, the toe of the Titan's boot caught on some rubble, and she sprawled out on the ground. She made a single weak attempt to push up to her elbows but dropped back down and fell still.

Seconds ticked by. A minute. Two. Three.

She didn't move again.

"Stay here," I told Hades, watching him sidelong until he nodded.

I moved forward, quiet and cautious, prepared to release the charged blast from my doru if the Titan made any attempt to strike, assuming she wasn't already dead. A low whine touched my ears when I was about ten steps away from the Titan.

I stopped and tilted my head to the side, listening. Was that *a whimper*?

The Titan was alive. And based on the sound she was making, she was in excruciating pain.

I inched forward, and when I was within leg's reach, I toed the containment cube away from her limp, charred hands. I took pity on her then. Not because she deserved a single ounce of my sympathy. But because *I* wasn't a monster.

"I can end your struggle," I said, echoing what another Titan had once told me, and angled the focus crystal at this Titan's head. I released the blast, and a poof of ash swallowed her head. Her lower body went limp.

I didn't wait for the dust to settle. I moved closer, crouched to pick up the orichalcum box, then stood and strode away. We just had one more thing to do, and then we could *finally* head back to the ship.

33

"Are you sure about this?" Hades asked, a lone consciousness orb cradled in his hand swirling with glittering electric-blue ribbons. My backup consciousness. Or, rather, the Cora half of my backup consciousness.

The thousands of visible consciousness orbs tucked into their individual recesses in the walls on either side of this corridor in the Vault of Souls sparkled in every imaginable color. I inhaled deeply and focused on the three consciousness orbs surrounding the empty recess awaiting the orb in Hades' hand. The sky-blue, tangerine, and sunny-yellow ribbons were all that remained of my mom, Raiden, and Emi.

Soon, I would join them. Sort of.

The instant Hades placed the orb in that cubby and uploaded *backup Cora* into the simulation, *I* would be locked out of the simulation forever. Gertie wouldn't allow for duplicate consciousnesses within the simulation. It would endanger the integrity of the entire program. Even though the orb contained *only* Cora, while *I* was still this strange

237

Cora-Peri hybrid, the Cora part of my mind would be flagged as a dupli-cate, and I would be denied entry.

Which meant this was it. My last chance to change my mind.

I locked stares with Hades and nodded once, telling him to proceed. And then I held my breath and watched as Hades placed the orb in the Vault of Souls, uploading *backup Cora* to the simulation.

34

Wʜᴇɴ I ᴏᴘᴇɴᴇᴅ ᴍʏ eyes and found myself standing in front of the boulder on the bluff at the edge of the woods on the Blackthorn estate, it took me eons to reorient myself to this new reality. The simulation. I was *in* the simulation.

Lazy waves crashed against the rocks below. A trio of gulls circled overhead, their squawking a comfort to my ears. The clouds in the overcast sky threatened rain, and the air—I closed my eyes and inhaled deeply—was fresh and crisp, with the briny tang that meant I was home.

"Cora."

My eyelids snapped open, and I whipped around to find Hades standing at the mouth of the trail, wearing his usual silver-gray tunic and pants, his pale hair gathered in a tie at the nape of his neck.

"What—" I squeezed my eyelids shut and shook my head. "Why am I here? What happened?" The last thing I remembered doing was sitting in a Genetec lab to make a backup of my consciousness. I had been preparing to head down to Othrys to search for Raiden, and—

I opened my eyes again and focused on Hades. "Where's Peri?" I asked, suddenly alarmed. I couldn't feel her within me. My fingers automatically sought my regulator, and I felt the pendant right where it always was, dangling from the chain around my neck.

Hades clasped his hands behind his back and watched me, his expression guarded. I could appreciate his otherworldly beauty, but I didn't feel the usual yearning to touch him. "We were unable to upload your dual consciousnesses as they were," he explained. "We were forced to *un*merge you and Peri."

My heart sank. "Is she *gone*?"

"Not exactly," Hades said, and the fact that he wasn't a wreck comforted me a bit.

"Is she in the simulation, too?" I asked.

Hades offered me a small smile. "It's better if you don't know."

"Oh," I said and frowned, my brows drawing together. "All right."

Hades turned to the side, extending his arm up the trail. "There are some people who would very much like to see you," he said.

"Who?" I asked, stepping closer to Hades. "What happened? Am I *dead*?" I figured I must have been dead if I was waking up in the simulation with no memory of how or why I was here. "Did we find Raiden?" I added. "Is he all right?"

"Again," Hades said, falling in step beside me on the trail, "it is better if you do not know the details. Many of your questions will be answered soon enough."

I looked around as we walked, taking survey of the physical sensations I felt with my virtual body. Noticing everything I heard and smelled. I had spent endless hours in VR, but it had never been like this. It had never felt *real*.

The silence stretched out between Hades and me, turning awkward in a way it had never been when Peri was a part of me. "So, um, are you in here, too?" I asked, finally finding something to say. "In the simulation, I mean."

Hades shook his head, and his stony expression told me he wouldn't offer any further explanation.

The forest debris littering the path crunched under our feet as we neared the edge of the woods, where the trail gave way to an expanse of lush green grass, and beyond the lawn, to Blackthorn Manor. I missed a step when I spotted the people seated in the teak Adirondack chairs on the back porch: my mom, Emi, and Raiden.

Hades caught my elbow to steady me but quickly let his hand fall away.

I walked ahead several steps while Hades hung back, pausing at the mouth of the trail. I was overcome with an unsettling combination of joy and sorrow. I was so happy to see them but so afraid of what their presence meant.

"Are they—" The word *dead* caught in my throat. I swallowed the rising grief and tried again. "Are they really here?" I asked, glancing back at Hades over my shoulder.

"They are," he said, moving forward to join me. "*And* they are expecting you."

I returned my attention to the trio on the deck.

Raiden spotted me first. He stood from his chair and hurried down the porch stairs, jogging across the lawn toward me. My mom and Emi followed at a slower pace.

I stepped onto the lawn, walking the first few steps, but soon I was running toward them. Toward *him*.

Raiden and I both slowed as we neared one another, breaths quickened by the burst of speed. The physical reaction seemed so odd, considering this was a *virtual* body. I dismissed the thought as soon as it entered my mind.

One last step and I was standing in front of Raiden. He wrapped his arms around me and lifted my feet off the ground. I squealed as he spun me in a full circle, and I was utterly breathless when he set my feet back down on the grass. His hand slid up along my spine and neck, his fingers sinking into my loose hair. I tilted my head back as he leaned in, stealing my breath all over again with an urgent kiss.

"All right, all right," my mom said as she and Emi joined us. "There'll be plenty of time for all that."

Laughing, Raiden released me, and I took a step backward. My mom moved in, throwing her arms around me and squeezing me tight. I reached for Emi, who hung back a step. She gripped my hand in greeting, then released it.

"Hades told us Peri is no longer with you," my mom said, loosening her embrace and pulling away enough that she could see my face. Her eyes searched mine. "Are you doing okay, sweetheart?"

I nodded, uncertain at first but more sure with each bob of my head. "It's weird," I said. "I remember having her with me—*being* her—but it's like she was a character in a video game. I was her, for a time, but she's *not me*." My brows bunched together, and I laughed, shaking my head. "I don't know if that makes any sense."

My mom rubbed her hands up and down my arms. "I think I understand," she said with a warm smile.

Behind me, Hades cleared his throat. "I should get back," he said.

I pulled away from my mom and turned to face him, all the awkwardness of our walk through the woods returning. I remembered loving him, but *I* didn't love him. The whole situation was extremely disorienting.

I stepped forward, then stopped, unable to close that final bit of distance between us. "Hades, I, um—" Unsure what to do, I thrust out my hand. "Thank you. For everything."

The corners of Hades' mouth twitched like he was holding back a smile. He stepped closer and wrapped his arms around me in an unexpectedly comforting embrace. "May you find peace here, Cora Blackthorn," Hades said, his voice rougher than before.

He released me and stepped back, nodding a silent farewell to each of us before turning away and vanishing.

I stared at the place where he had been, wondering if I would ever see him again.

A slender arm curved around my shoulders before I could delve too deeply into the what-ifs of my new situation. "Come on," my mom said, tucking me close against her side and turning me around to guide me toward the house. "I made a pie. It should be cool by now."

My eyebrows shot up my forehead. "*You* made a pie?"

She chuckled, Emi and Raiden walking alongside us. "What can I say?" my mom said. "I caught the cooking bug on the *Elysium*."

I guffawed. "That wasn't cooking!"

"But it made me *want* to cook," she explained.

I eyed her sidelong. "Did you follow a recipe?"

"Uh-huh," she said, her voice rising in pitch as she averted her gaze.

Emi snorted delicately. "She *read* a recipe," Emi said. "Does that count?"

I exchanged an amused glance with Raiden, and his hand found mine, our fingers threading together. I couldn't remember the last time I had felt this happy. This safe. This *at peace*.

I gave his hand a squeeze, then said, "I guess we're about to find out."

35

HADES PULLED HIS HAND away from the consciousness orb tucked into its recess in the wall in this part of the Vault of Souls and gazed at the glittering electric-blue ribbons for several heartbeats. Was he saying his last goodbye to her, that isolated part of my backup consciousness?

I shut down the holographic screen hovering above my holoband and lowered my arm. Tears coated my cheeks, and my heart ached with longing after watching the reunion within the simulation. How strange that I now existed in two places at once. There was *backup Cora* within the simulation, and *me*, the same strange Cora-Peri hybrid, out here.

Hades exhaled a long, drawn-out sigh, then straightened his shoulders and turned to face me. "Are you doing all right?"

A hollow laugh shook my chest, and I offered him a sad excuse for a smile.

Hades moved closer, raising his hands to cradle either side of my jaw. He tilted my head back, angling my face toward his, and leaned in. He kissed first one cheekbone, then the other, before pressing his lips gently to mine. His kiss was salty with my tears.

"I am honored by this sacrifice," he said, pulling back a few inches.

I wouldn't lie to him and tell him it was nothing. It was *worth it*, but it wasn't nothing. After all we had been through on Othrys, I knew where I belonged. Who I—this strange hybrid person formed from the merging of two selves—belonged with. Hades was my person. He was my matching puzzle piece, with all the right notches and grooves and jagged edges.

But when I had been *just* Cora, I had fit perfectly with another person. With Raiden. I had feared that the what-if of a possible future with Raiden would eat away at me, eventually eroding my edges until I no longer fit with Hades. So, I had asked Hades to separate the Cora part of my backup consciousness and upload her to the simulation to be with her people. They were *my* people, too, but *she* was the version of me they needed.

The separation procedure hadn't been a sure thing, but it had worked. *Backup Cora*—*just* Cora—would live on in the simulation with Raiden, my mom, and Emi, while I—the original Cora-Peri hybrid—remained on the outside, the simulation forever closed to me.

I would never be with them again. I could watch them on a screen, as I had their reunion, but I would never speak to them directly. Never hold them. They were beyond my reach, now, in the simulation, and after. When the *Elysium* reached Terra, they would be reborn together to live out their second lives on that new, peaceful world.

Hades and I, however, had chosen not to resurrect. We would live out this cycle together, and it would be our last lifetime. And hopefully, our best lifetime.

Hades' hands slid down from my face, following the line of my neck, skimming over my shoulders, and gliding down my arms to take my hands in his. "Do you regret it?" he asked, glancing to the side, to the orb containing *backup Cora*. She was half of me, but now she felt like an entirely different person.

I gazed down at our joined hands. "It's funny," I said, my voice hushed. "Part of me wonders if the ancient Greeks weren't onto something with our story—like they had tapped into some prophetic force that could foresee our future." The Olympians didn't believe in such things, but they had yet to unlock all the universe's secrets. Perhaps this was one of them.

"What do you mean?" Hades asked.

I smiled down at our hands, then raised my gaze to meet his. "They spoke of Persephone living divided, split between two worlds—the world of the living and the underworld, the land of the dead." I glanced at the orb containing a duplicate of the Cora part of me, watching the electric-blue ribbons whirl within.

"And now I'm doing just that. Part of me is in there—*living*, for all intents and purposes. But this part of me is out here." I swept my gaze up and around the Vault of Souls, only a fraction of the consciousness orbs stored within its walls visible from our vantage point. "Watching over the dead." I returned my focus to Hades. "With you."

Hades was quiet, his uncertainty written all over his face. I hadn't answered his question about regretting my decision to upload *backup Cora* to the simulation. But even if I had answered him, if I told him I didn't regret my decision to lock myself out of the simulation and effectively bind my fate with his, he wouldn't have believed me. Not fully.

I pulled my right hand free from Hades' hold and raised it to trace my finger around my new regulator. It was a hand-me-down from one of the Zari's Amazons who had perished during the pirate attack. It didn't have the sentimental value of the other—the one that had saved our lives—which had been a gift from Hades, having originally belonged to his mom, Rhea. I deactivated this regulator, staring down at the device as the subtle amber glow gave way to brilliant, electric-blue light.

Peering at Hades, I drew his hand up and pressed it flat against my chest, his palm covering the pendant, and opened myself to him. His eyes widened as my emotions flowed through the regulator and into him. As he gained access to my whole self. To my every thought and emotion. To my every hope and fear. To all that was *me*.

"I love you, Hades," I told him, staring into those infinite ice-blue irises, letting him feel my certainty. My honesty. "And I don't regret a single thing where you're concerned."

Hades' lips parted, his expression one of pure wonder.

"Well," I added, a smirk twisting my lips as I thought of all the time we had missed out on. All those years—literal lifetimes—where we could have explored each other's deepest, darkest desires. "Maybe one thing . . "

A flush crept up Hades' neck, and his pupils dilated, lust darkening his eyes. "I think we can make up for that," he said, his voice deeper and rougher than before.

"Do you have anywhere you need to be right now?" I asked. "The Bridge? Or a lab?" I knew he was itching to study my DNA to understand why *I* was able to access the psychic energy produced by the fungus like a Titan when no other non-Tsakali psychics could—human or Olympian.

Hades shook his head. "Nothing pressing."

My smirk widened to a wicked grin, and my voice turned husky. "Good."

36

I SUPPRESSED A GAG and turned partially away as Fiona cracked open the chest cavity of the headless, charred Titan stretched out on the exam table. Hades and I had circled back in the *Argo* to retrieve her remains before flying away from Othrys at Fiona's behest.

"It's just a machine," Fiona said, eyeing me like *I* was the weird one when *she* was the one who was perfectly happy going elbow-deep into what looked—and smelled—like a horribly burned corpse.

I attempted to watch, but my stomach roiled, and I turned my back to her. "Sorry," I mumbled. "Maybe I should come back after—"

"No need," Fiona chirped. There was a squelching sound, followed by a sharp snap. "Got it." More squelching as she dragged her arm out of the Titan's torso.

I glanced over my shoulder, watching out of the corner of my eye as she pulled the Titan's CPU free. It was kind of like peeking out from behind a pillow to watch a horror movie. The distance made it *slightly* less disturbing.

"So, are you going to go back to Peri?" Fiona asked, stepping around me, her long gloves stained red up to her elbows.

"I'm sorry," I said, my brow furrowing. "What?"

"Your name." Fiona dunked the Titan's CPU into a tub filled with a clear solution and cleaned it carefully. "Are you going to start going by Peri? Now that there's another Cora in the sim?"

Fiona pulled the CPU out of the tub and dried it off as she carried it over to her workstation. She had built a human-Olympian hybrid computer, which could interface directly with Gertie, tapping into the AI's excess processing power and exponentially speeding up every test, model, or other task Fiona performed.

"Oh, um . . ." I frowned and shook my head. "I don't think so. *I'm* still Cora, too. It's hard to explain, but I think that because I lived as *Cora* for so long in this body that it would feel weird to go by anything else."

"Coolio," Fiona said as she peeled off her gloves, then attached a cord from the CPU and set it down beside the one from the pirate Titan, which she had already attached and analyzed. "Gertie, please analyze the new Titan CPU, cross-referencing with the original," Fiona said, swiping her fingers over the screen of her tablet.

A holoscreen appeared, hovering above the workstation, displaying graphs and charts that meant nothing to me. But Fiona stared at the readings, mesmerized by whatever she saw there. With the way her brain worked, sometimes it seemed like *she* wasn't entirely human either.

"What exactly are you looking for?" I asked. She had sounded excited when she called me down here. I, however, had *not* been excited to be dragged out of bed—cough, *with Hades*—to dissect a Titan's corpse.

"I had a thought," Fiona murmured. Her eyes shifted this way and that as she scanned the readings. She didn't explain further.

"Which was?" I prompted.

Fiona blinked and finally focused on me. "Was what?"

"Your thought," I said. "What was it?"

"Oh, right." Fiona let out one of those too-shrill laughs that made me think she was due for another mandatory sleep break. "I remembered what you said about the pirate Titan—that she had a conscience and that the other Tsakali wanted to destroy her because of it."

"Uh-huh . . ." I crossed my arms over my chest and leaned back against the neighboring worktable.

"So that got me thinking," Fiona explained. "If we had another Titan to compare our unicorn to, maybe we could isolate whatever it was within her coding that made her so unique."

I frowned and narrowed my eyes, understanding what she wanted to do, but not *why*. "To what end?" I asked.

Fiona blinked and appeared slightly taken aback that I hadn't connected the dots on my own. "To end the war," she said, her tone ringing with an implied *duh*.

"Explain it to me like I'm an idiot," I suggested.

"Um . . ." Fiona drew her lower lip between her teeth and furrowed her brow. "Okay, so it's like this," she said. "The Olympians have been focused on destroying the Tsakali, but what if there was another way to end this?"

I snorted a laugh. "I hardly think diplomacy is going to work."

Excitement lit Fiona's emerald irises. "Because they're machines," she said, hand gestures getting bigger as she really got going with her explanation. "Because they don't have a *conscience* to appeal to. No sense of empathy or compassion. They don't care about the destruction they spread across the universe. Because right now, their highest drive is to consume so they can expand. So they can dominate. So they can be indestructible and ensure the survival of their kind. *But—"* She paused, lowering her chin.

"But?" I asked.

"But," she repeated, "what if they *did* have a conscience we could appeal to?" She raised her eyebrows. "What if they *were* capable of empathy? What if we could transform them into creatures who *did* care?"

I pushed off the edge of the table and stood up, my arms slackening as my mind raced. "Are you saying you could replicate whatever it was that made the pirate Titan *feel*?"

"I'm saying I can *try*," Fiona said. "They're just computers, right?" She stepped closer, her stare burning with a manic light. It was *definitely* time for Fiona to take a break. "If I can make a virus that would spread the pirate Titan's unique condition to the rest of her kind, we can *infect* each and every one of them with *a soul.*"

I licked my lips, my heart beating faster as some of Fiona's excitement rubbed off on me. It was insane what she was suggesting. Completely insane. Yet, so far as I knew, it was totally different from anything the Olympians had tried to do to defeat the Tsakali before.

"We don't need to kill them to end this war," Fiona said. "We just need to make them feel."

Thanks for reading! You've reached the end of *BLOOD OF THE BROKEN* (Atlantis Legacy, #5). Cora's adventures will continue in *RISE OF THE REVENANTS*, the sixth and final book in the Atlantis Legacy.

You can read the four bonus and extended scenes on my Patreon. Two of the four stories are public and free to read for everyone, including a spicy extended love scene from chapter 24 and a bonus epilogue from simulation-Cora's POV. Definitely check those out, even if you're not a Patron. They're definitely worth the read!

www.patreon.com/lindseysparks

You can read the prequel to the Atlantis Legacy, *SACRIFICE OF THE SINNERS*, for free by subscribing to my newsletter. You'll also gain access to more exclusive freebies, stay apprised of new releases, and receive previews, updates, and other book-related announcements in your inbox once or twice a month.

www.authorlindseysparks.com/join-newsletter

ABOUT LINDSEY SPARKS

Lindsey Sparks lives her life with one foot in a book—so long as that book transports her to a magical world or bends the rules of science. Her novels, from Post-apocalyptic (writing as Lindsey Fairleigh to Time Travel Romance, always offer up a hearty dose of unreality, along with plenty of history, intrigue, adventure, and romance.

When she's not working on her next novel, Lindsey spends her time hanging out with her two little boys, working in her garden, or playing board games with her husband. She lives in the Pacific Northwest with her family and their small pack of cats and dogs.

lindseysparks.com

SOCIAL MEDIA: @authorlindseysparks

www.ingramcontent.com/pod-product-compliance
Lightning Source LLC
Chambersburg PA
CBHW021125190726
48288CB00008B/2510